FLAMINGO
BOOK OF NEW SCOTTISH
WRITING
1997

Introduction by Douglas Gifford

Flamingo
An Imprint of HarperCollinsPublishers

Flamingo
An Imprint of HarperCollins*Publishers*
77–85 Fulham Palace Road,
Hammersmith, London w6 8jb

First published by Flamingo 1997
9 8 7 6 5 4 3 2 1

The Publisher acknowledges the financial assistance of the
Scottish Arts Council in the publication of this volume

A catalogue record for this book
is available from the British Library

ISBN 0 00 655050 9

Set in Postscript Linotype New Baskerville by
Rowland Phototypesetting Ltd,
Bury St Edmunds, Suffolk

Printed and bound in Great Britain by
Caledonian International Book Manufacturing Ltd, Glasgow

FLAMINGO
BOOK OF NEW SCOTTISH
WRITING
1997

CONTENTS

Introduction

Since this annual series began back in 1973 (when Neil Paterson and myself worked through submissions for that first collection) the Scottish short story has changed in a number of striking ways. Outstandingly, it has reorientated itself away from the tradition, so strong in Scottish fiction from Scott and Hogg to Linklater and George Mackay Brown, of a narrative which drew its strength from rural landscapes and seascapes, and from legend and myth. A feature of this tradition was its balancing of the claims of possible and mutually exclusive supernatural and psychological interpretations, so that readers had to choose between identifying diabolic forces influencing events, or reading the central and tormented protagonist as victim of a crippling inheritance of religious and social repression. The tradition which produced such classics as Stevenson's 'Thrawn Janet' and Linklater's 'Sealskin Trousers' still persists; but traditional supernaturalism has by and large given way to a new kind of magic realism in the work of writers like Gray, Lochhead, Morgan, Banks, and many of the contemporary novelists, in which the mundane concerns of ordinary human beings matter, and if magic is involved, it's the magic that tinges the realism of ordinary people's lives. The themes of today's fiction are reflected in this collection. Personal and family crises, moments of realization of where one fits – or doesn't fit – amongst friends and community, yearnings for another time and another place to live in, and – outstandingly – the realization from the point of view of women, children and other underprivileged outsiders of the many traditionally Scottish (and often international) repressive and unfair family and social backgrounds: these are the signs that new writing refuses to accept old dispensations, that complex and immediate problems call for sophisticated consideration and therapeutic treatment. For many of these stories carry the hallmark of painful personal experience. One of the significant results of the immense burgeoning of writers' circles in Scotland and Britain has been the breaking down of barriers to self-expression, analysis, and the transformation of pain into art, and a reading of these fine stories – chosen from a huge entry of comparable quality – cannot help but see patterns which tell much about the new Scotlands in which most of these writers live and work.

It's worth grouping these stories according to their main focus. Predominantly they are about times of crisis or recognition. Of course, all good short stories focus on a telling or turning moment, but somehow these Scottish-orientated stories seem distinctive in their acute and localized concern with loss of love, community, and place. Personal pain is in almost every story, and in seeking a rough rationale for the volume it is striking to see how naturally these accounts of moments of recognition of personal tragedy and comedy arrange themselves into strata – children's perspectivves, first-person adult views, familial or group crises, and recognition of the predicament of the outsider – which add up to a kind of synchronic, snapshot glimpse of the range of the plurality of contemporary Scottish life, complete with international variations and comparisons, and articulated in the varieties of language and register which modern Scotland rightly relishes as an enrichment of its culture.

The use of the child's view of adult events is an old device, but in the hands of the writers here it is exploited to powerful new effect. Greig's 'Porky Pig and Fando Fillamon' is perhaps the most traditional of these in its poetry of childhood, with its timeless perception of the class scapegoat, snivelling Porky, and the class outsider, the cool and left-alone gypsy boy, Fando. Greig is one of Scotland's finest poets, and this bittersweet mixture of cruelty and love outstandingly exemplifies the way the writers in this collection refuse the glib and deliberately confuse happiness and despair. McIntyre's 'The Curam' moves to the islands to tease out the mixed meanings of its title, an old term for revivalist ecstasy. Marsali discovers the tensions of response in her small community to the Quintons, the newly-arrived bakers who want her to discover Christ. Once again, the child finds that community is simultaneously close and cruel, as does young Ella in Gowans's 'Manitoba', her idealistic dream of another time and another place broken by the capriciousness of parents and circumstances. Anne Donovan's wee Mary (or Merry, as she rightly sees herself) in 'Hieroglyphics' cleverly exposes community and class tensions through a first-person account of subtle revenge told in vivid Glaswegian; the child who has been let down by a system insensitive to her real imaginative abilities; a system which condemns her as writing badly because she speaks badly, discovers the possibilities of Egyptian-style pictograms, and leaves the reader, and the school inspector who will assess her picture-essay, to judge the system and the girl. And two stories bring out the latent darkness of this group: Heyman's 'Chasing Stallions' with its horrific child's view of the macho sexuality and incestuous violence of the war-scarred policeman father seeing death and family tragedy through harshly poetic imagery; and Roberts's 'Goodbye, Robbie Tuesday', with its tragedy in the accidental death of the boys' father after a family argument, but with elements of catharsis and implied healing where the former story hinted at lifelong trauma.

This thematic view of our brave new worlds is then

continued in a series of stories of older disillusion. The family – or more often the broken family – is still the place of damage, but older witnesses bear more complex testimonies, as in Colins's 'Tangerines', where middle-aged Kathie has her mid-life crisis, breaks from her pot-bellied musician lover and sets out to abduct the child she lost to adoption. The realization of her own pathetic stupidity, together with the merciless depiction of the hor-rifically spoiled daughter, make this one of the most pain-ful stories of the collection – and yet somehow, like so many of the writers here, Colins turns tragedy into forgive-ness and reconciliation. Faber's 'Missing Photographs' has likewise the pain of family breakup and its aftermath; the unnamed son, searching for a photo of his Polish father to send to Polish relatives, rediscovers possibilities of imagination and affection denied to his embittered mother. No story captures the possibilities of redemptive imagination more effectively than Soltysek's 'Teuchter Dancing When the Lights Go Out'; here is the triumph of spirit over death, in the short, intense expression of a credo of life-in-death from a paralysed man using memory to dance, as his limbs one-by-one switch off. But there are darker resolutions to these stories of familial and group recognition. Aboulela's 'Souvenirs' strands its Arab North Sea oil-rigger between Aberdeen and Khartoum, caught forever between Scottish wife and values and the reproach of his mother and sister, together with memories of smells and skies of both countries. In 'Those American Thoughts' McWilliam strands her gallus young Craig in even more debateable land, since he hasn't even been to the America which he uses to distance himself from his unhappy girlfriend, as he invents ambitions and experi-ences to dupe her in the Edwardian Bar at Lily Langtry's in Aberdeen. These quiet predicaments and betrayals seem to be perpetuated in Pickin's 'Flight of Fancy', in which Ailsa identifies with the remote, elusive heron as a means of reconciling herself to her worldly, down-to-earth marriage. But Pickin takes the apparently gentle Ailsa to heights of fierce resentment; the heron's capture has been the last straw, and the rest is bizarre tragedy.

One of the results of increased familiarity with these stories is the realization that, for all their variety of ways of expressing their often shared themes, they shade into each other to create a striking overall effect of sympathy for, and empathy with, outsiders. From the children so often pushed to run away or to quiet disappointment or rebellion, and from the adults traumatized or damaged by past familial disintegration, most of the stories discussed so far suggest a Scotland and Britain under siege from the pressure of emotional tension, materialism, and physical separation. Perhaps the Scottish writer emphasizes this more, simply because – as the tradition of Scottish litera-ture shows repeatedly – community and mutual depen-dency used to matter so much more than in most cultures. The pain of loss is perhaps greater in our northern, ances-tor, family and memory haunted country. Whatever the reason, the final grouping of stories takes the idea of the social misfit, the family outsider, to sometimes grotesque conclusions. No more grotesque conclusion can be found than that of the cheerfully deranged old woman in Hills's 'Pictures of Ivy'; the juxtaposition of her sheer goodwill and her loneliness is a painful reminder to a society which already knows its abandonment of too many like her, and Ivy's shocking exit from this society is at once brave, appal-ling and wonderful. Two authors, Spence and Falla, locate their outsiders in exotic locations far from Scotland in 'My son, My Son' and 'Raise a Glass to Mr Sing' respectively. In the first Icarus tells the inside story of lustful Queen Pasiphae and the Minotaur in Crete, and how he and his son sought to avoid the endless fate of the exploited; in the second a Scottish tourist in the East discovers the pathetic yet endlessly optimistic and resourceful Mr Sing, a guide of hilarious eccentricity and yet archetypal human endeavour. Misfits have to be astonishingly resourceful, say these stories; survival is a day-to-day business, fraught with tragedy. And two stories bring us back to misfits more familiar, in Fitzpatrick's 'A Shared Experience', and McGill's 'Maureen and Bonzo and Joe'. Fitzpatrick sensitively portrays the insensitive Margaret, met in a maternity ward in one of those hospital encounters which brings together classes and types which would never normally meet. Margaret presumably wouldn't be a misfit back where she comes from; but the story suggests that the way some people and communities fit together leaves them, in their harsh and foreshortened spectrum of feeling and development, unfit for any chance of fulfilled life. Margaret's farewell 'bugger off' to the friendly enquiry regarding her baby gives the other side of working-class solidarity, as does McGill's graphic picture of gallus Maureen and her Rottweiler Bonzo, as he does the business on the floor of the cafe in the Princes Square shopping precinct. Maureen's day is funny and coarse, but her tragedy with mean-tempered wee Joe and her squalid life is relieved only by her genuine affection for her big dog – and perhaps by death. Such grim humour is probably the most traditional aspect of the volume, and for me the climatic story, emphasizing traditional features, yet breaking new ground, exploiting possibilities of language and reflecting on the contemporary transformations of Scotland, is Aberdein's ribald, gutsy tale of smeddum and modern alienation, the magnificently eccentric dialect portrait of the extraordinary Shetland fisherman, 'Spermy McClung'. Spunky he is indeed, and a whale of a man in his cowboy swagger, his willingness to take on all authorities, and his Scandinavian, saga-like understatement in action and voice when he loses his arm in that ghastly accident with the trawling gear. People and life, Scottish and universal, are what these stories are about, and nowhere more so than in this emblematic tale which tells us that Scottish character thrives even as it doesn't bother too much about being Scottish.

These stories are primarily interconnected in their relation to broad themes, and only secondarily in their depiction of Scotland. They don't concern themselves much with history, or even the recent past, and they don't bother much with an awareness of those elements of the Scottish literary traditions such as the supernatural, or an emphasis on folk in a landscape who are aware of the rhythms of season and nature. Eleven are set in Scotland, from Shetland to the Borders, the inner Hebrides to Glasgow; three are set in Scotland, but dominated by dreams of somewhere abroad, somewhere tantalizingly different; while four are set in places not at all Scottish. It's a proportioning which seems to me to speak for contemporary Scottish eclecticism, and one which welcomes new and different races and values. What made the choosing of these stories from a wealth of comparable talent so fascinating for Robyn Marsack, Mandy Kirkby and myself was the multiplicity of voices speaking confidently and with sophistication about fundamental concerns of self, family, and society. Long may this annual volume continue to represent contemporary Scotlands and beyond.

This volume was the last to be presided over by the Scottish Arts Council's Walter Cairns, who retired in 1996.

DOUGLAS GIFFORD 1996

FLAMINGO
BOOK OF NEW SCOTTISH
WRITING

1997

MAUREEN AND BONZO
AND JOE

John McGill

She took Bonzo to the Princes Square Precinct, where he wasn't allowed. At the door she hooked on his leash. Inside, some people gave them looks but nobody said anything, that's the beauty of Rottweilers.

On the see-through lift he started keiching in the corner and an old woman in a fur coat said that was disgraceful, they had no right, but she just ignored her and Bonzo just keiched and keiched. He still wasn't finished at the top, and he was doing it among the tables outside the fancy café when a security man came up. He said they had to get the hell out, dogs were barred, and she could get a summons and a two-hundred-pound fine for letting him shite on everything like that.

She said, 'What am I supposed to do, stitch his arse up?'

The security man nearly laughed, so she knew he was OK, really. He helped her to get Bonzo onto the escalator and came down with them to make sure the big paws didn't get stabbed on the prongs at the bottom. They had a good laugh about the two hundred, but he told her it was no joke, she wouldn't be the first, she should make tracks pronto pronto.

'He done it in the lift as well,' she said, and the security man looked up at the skylight and said, 'Oh Christ.'

She held out her packet of Dorchester Mild and he took one and put it in his top pocket for later.

'He cost me two hundred and fifty,' she said. 'He's a pedigree.'

The security man gave Bonzo a quick pat on the head, and Bonzo cringed. 'Aye, a pedigree shitebag,' the man said.

The sun was bright and hurt her eyes and she felt dizzy among the big buildings in Buchanan Street, so she sat on a bench and told Bonzo to sit, but he just stood leaning on her leg. They were next to a big thing, a big black lump of iron on a stone plinth. She liked it because some-body had scratched 'WULLIE'S DA DONE THIS' on the plinth, with an arrow pointing up to the thing. Two people were looking at it and talking about it. There was a man in a camel coat and a red scarf, and a woman who looked like one of the dummies in the Edinburgh Wool Shop. The woman was pointing at a bit of the thing high up, and they were laughing.

'Wullie's da done it,' Maureen said.

The woman stopped laughing and gave her a look and said, 'Pardon?'

Maureen pointed at the scratching. 'Wullie's da, see? It says it.'

The man saw the scratching and pointed it out to the woman. She shook her head and said to the man, 'I'm sorry,' and he smiled down at her and kissed the top of her head. He was English.

Bonzo had a real name, printed on a long bit of yellow paper that she kept in her purse: Herzog Aldolphus Langenhals der Vierte. Young Andy had forked out the two hundred and fifty when Big Andy died and she was left on her own. 'That's instead of my da,' he said.

4

'Set me back two hundred and fifty, the wee bastard.'

Wee was a laugh. Bonzo had feet like sideboards even then, and now they were like caravans. He had a big long tail that took away some of the Rottweiler look; people usually snipped their tails and made them look frightening and wicked, pure muscle and teeth.

Wee Joe had only three teeth and he was as manky as an old doormat, but he kept Bonzo in his place. One growl from him and Bonzo was under the table howling. Joe had always been short-tempered, but after Big Andy died he went really terrible, he just bit and snapped at everything.

An old dirty man sat down beside her on the bench, looking for a fag.

'That's a great dog you've got there,' he said. 'That's a real stoater.'

'Aye,' she said. She gave him a Dorchester Mild and took one for herself and lit them.

'He's a pedigree. Cost over two hundred pound,' she said.

'Christ, aye,' he said. 'You can see that a mile away, he's a real stoater. Bet you he takes a bit of feeding.'

She nodded. 'You can say that again. Costs a fortune.'

He asked for fifty pence for a cup of tea, but she told him she only had fifty pence for the subway, and that was her lot till Tuesday. He believed her.

'You going on the subway then?'

'Aye.'

'Jesus. That's a thing I've never been on, that subway.'

'We like it,' she said. She patted Bonzo's head, rubbed his ears. 'Don't we, son?'

'I've never been on it,' he said again. 'That you going home for your dinner, like?'

'No, we're not going anywhere. We just sit on it and go round a few times. He likes it.'

'What? You just go round and round – just back to where you started?'

'Aye. It passes the time.'

'That's a thing I've never been on, never in my life. Do they let dogs on?'

'I don't know. They let him on.' She pulled Bonzo's right ear. 'They let you on, don't they? They don't say boo to you.'

'I don't blame them. I'd like a wee run myself – what is it? Fifty pence?'

'Aye. It's fifty pence whatever distance you go, you can sit on it the whole day if you want.'

He was impressed. 'That right? Fifty pence for a whole day? Christ, that's a bargain. Wish I had it. I'd come for a wee run with you, just for a laugh. Maybe next time.'

'Aye,' she said.

'What about that, eh? I come for a wee run with you, round and back to where we started?'

'No bother.'

He touched her knee. 'What would your man say to that, eh? You and me having a run round and round on the old Clockwork Orange?'

'My man's dead,' she said.

'Oh. Sorry to hear that, sorry about that.'

'He's been dead two year. He used to like it as well, him and me used to go round and round, but now it's just Bonzo and me.'

Hearing his name, Bonzo looked up.

'I'll tell you the truth,' the man said, 'I don't even know where it goes to, the bastard. Where does it go to?'

'I don't know,' she said. 'We just go round.'

She stood up and tugged on Bonzo's leash. The man

told her to have a good run, and she gave him another Dorchester Mild and said cheerio.

The subway was quiet. Middle of the morning, middle of the week. A few students got on at Cowcaddens, two boys and two girls, and one of the boys patted Bonzo's head, to show off to the girls. Bonzo tried to sit on the seat at first but it was too narrow, so he jumped off and sat at her leg for a couple of stations, then he flopped down on his belly. She always went on the Inner Circle, because it sounded safer. She liked getting to the stations south of the river – West Street, Shields Road, Cessnock, Ibrox. She'd never been in any of these places, never even really heard of any of them except Ibrox, and that was worse than Hell, that was no-go; so it felt like being somewhere. One or two other people came on, but they just sat and read papers or stared into space, nobody talked. She felt like smoking a Dorchester Mild, but that had started a fight with a woman last time, and this time she wasn't in the mood, she was saving her energy.

It was busier when she got out again at St Enoch's. Nearly dinner time. There were three left in the Dorchester Mild packet. She sat on a bench and smoked one, then she lit another one to smoke while she walked along the street to Rentaset. When she reached the door she took out the last one and lit it, and dropped the packet on the pavement.

'I'll need to get some fags, son,' she said to Bonzo. She told him to stay at the door. She took three big draws on the Dorchester Mild and took a brown envelope from her coat pocket and walked into the shop. A tall thin young man came up to her. On his pullover he had a badge that said 'Neil' in fancy computer letters.

'How can I help you, madam?' he said. There was a smile, but his voice sounded irritated.

7

She handed him the envelope, showing him the name on the front. 'You can stop writing to him,' she said.

He read the name. 'Mr McDonald. So are you Mrs McDonald, madam?'

'Aye, and he's dead.' She had raised her voice, and a man who was playing with the computers on a table near them looked up and traded sympathetic looks with Neil.

'Oh,' Neil said. 'I see. I'm very sorry to hear that.'

'So am I,' she said.

He motioned her towards a counter. 'Would you like to just come over here and we'll see what we can do?' he said.

'I've got to go home and get my dinner,' she told him, but she went to the counter.

He took out the letter. It was dated 7 January. He looked at his watch, checking that the date was now 28 March. The letter was printed in red.

'So the problem is whether you want to keep the equipment or return it?'

'No. The problem is I don't want these letters coming to the house – my man's dead.'

She stressed the last word, it always made them nervous. She could see him wondering what to say next. He looked around for help before he spoke, but everybody was busy.

'So have you had a few of these letters, Mrs McDonald?'

'A few? I had plenty. I have hundreds of them. I could paper the house with them, so I could.'

'Oh.' His face was getting red. 'Well, I think maybe you might want to speak to Mr Clark about this – he's the manager.'

'All right, well, I'll speak to him, but I've got to get home for my dinner.'

While he was finding the manager she watched the television sets that were all showing the same picture, with no sound, thirty times over, in three rows of ten.

The manager's badge said 'Mr T. Clark' and below that, 'Manager'. He asked what the problem was. He was pleased to get the chance to show off in front of Neil, you could see that on his face. He was small and fat, like herself, and he had steel-rimmed glasses and a grey moustache and a white bald head. She just gave him a look then turned back to the TVs.

'How is it they're all different?' she asked him.

He looked at the sets. Ann and Nick were on a sofa, talking to somebody who was always on chat shows, a woman with a big mouth and teeth. They were all laughing at some joke, but you couldn't tell what it was because the sound was turned down on all the sets.

Mr Clark grinned narrowly. 'Different?' he said.

'Look,' she said. 'Some of them they look like niggers and others they're like ghosts.'

'That's the colour adjustment,' he said. 'You adjust it to suit your taste.'

'But what one's the right colour?'

'It depends on taste,' he said. 'People see things differently.'

She shrugged and softly said, 'Stupid.' Then she turned to settle the business with him. He asked her if it was a problem with keeping up the rental and she said no, she wasn't interested in the rental, she didn't have the video and the telly in her house, they were Big Andy's things, it was him took to do with everything like that and he'd been dead two years. He asked her what had happened to the equipment. She could see young Neil nearly laughing behind his back. She said maybe Big Andy had put it back. The only thing she had was an old black-and-white portable – and no video, she never knew how to work them. He said they had no record of it coming back and she said that was their problem, not hers, it was over two years ago and she was fed up with the hassle and if there was another letter she would write to the *Daily Record* and Radio Clyde and STV, they liked stories about shops that hassled poor widows.

In the end he gave her a pat on the shoulder and told her not to worry, he would keep the letter and sort things out for her. Neil was smiling at her now and this time it was real.

Bonzo stood up when she came out of the shop. She patted him and said, 'Dinner time, son. Another five minutes and I could have got a washing machine off that wee bastard.'

Bonzo found an old mutton bone and carried it all the way to the close, even though she told him to drop it. Bones were the one thing he was brave about. It was a long walk and her chest was heaving, but she had a new packet of Dorchester Mild that she got at the Paki's and a single fish from the Chicken Bar and she was feeling happy and looking forward to a sit down and a cup of tea.

But it was no rest for the wicked, as usual. Bonzo still had the bone when they went in, and the minute Joe saw it he was at it like a wee manky black tiger. With just the three teeth he had no chance of getting it off Bonzo that way. Bonzo just lifted his head and he had to let go.

'Stop that, you two,' she said. 'Give me peace.'

But they weren't listening. Joe did his usual – he got Bonzo by the leg. Normally that was enough to send Bonzo scampering under the table, but not now, not with a big mutton bone that still had meat on it. Bonzo dropped the bone and growled. Joe grabbed it in his gums and tried to get off his mark, but Bonzo put his big paw on Joe's back and held him down, then got a grip on the bone again. He was raging, but he was still too scared to pull it hard because that would have hurt Joe, that would have been his last three teeth out the game. So he just hung on and Joe pulled and the pair of them growled. It was pure stalemate. Maureen got mad.

'Jesus Christ, you two, can you give me peace?'

They ignored her again, so she grabbed an old *Evening Times* that was lying on the couch and rolled it up and waved it. That was another thing that Bonzo was usually scared of, but this time he just let her wave it, he just hung on to his bone.

'Right,' she said, 'I'll settle this once and for all. That bloody bone's going in the bin.'

The bit of bone between their noses was as wide as her hand. She grabbed it and gave a jerk, but they were ready. They shifted their grips to pull against her as well as against each other. She sat on the carpet and settled in for a real war.

'You wee bastards,' she said. 'I'll kill the two of you.'

Bonzo and her were much the same weight, but Joe was the most vicious, so it was a hard fight. She was gasping and trying to laugh at the same time. She could hardly breathe and there was a tight feeling in her chest, so she let go of the bone. The surprise made them stop growling, but they hung on to their ends even though their ears went up, listening, when she spoke.

She leaned back, taking her weight on her right hand and putting her left up to her chest, just below her throat.

'Oof,' she said.

THOSE AMERICAN
THOUGHTS

Candia McWilliam

'There's places over there you'd not thank me if I took you right enough when all's said and done. The people are different, not like here. They're different. They'd cross the road before they would talk to you on the public street. And it's five highways wide.' Craig soaked up a good bit of his lager.

'The street?' Elise fiddled with the kirby in her hair. It was chosen from a selection at Boots to be the shade closest to the colour of her hair. Her bobcut was dark brown with a halo where the pearlized restaurant lamp over their table was reflected.

'The road.'

'Is the street not the road then?'

'Not the way it is here. And no way is the road the street. They use roads for getting places, not for living in. If you're walking along the cars'll give you a wide berth because anyone walking along must be mad. Or not have a car, which is the same as mad, right enough. There it's. There's your food. Looks warm any road.'

Craig was having a bad evening. He'd come all the way North back home to Aberdeen to let Elise know he wanted out from their engagement and he was giving a talk about attitudes to vehicles in the United States, where, he'd given it out, he'd been these last two months. On an engineering job, another lie. They couldn't get enough bridges, he'd said. Over water; inland waterways. Great demand for Scottish know-how. The Scots had a name for bridges.

In actual fact, he'd been washing up in a tourist hotel on Loch Lomondside, with occasional bar work after the last bus took away the nonresident staff. There'd been a large number of Americans at the Girning Stramlach Inn, right enough. And he must stop saying right enough. His mouth was operating against his brain. It did that around the women. Then again, he'd been with Elise seven years, since she was fourteen, so he owed her the gentle letdown.

They were in the Edwardian Bar at Lillie Langtry's. She was having a mince masala pitta surprise and Craig had stuck with what he knew and gone for a mixed grill, not noticing until too late that it'd come under 'Vegetarian'. So his plate looked like what the papers showed found in old burial sites to prove that Caledonian man had once been a grain eater or what have you. He'd catch up on his meat intake with a poke of scratchings after he'd fetched Elise off his conscience.

The lights were low, the music soupy. In the corner a group of big men emptied pints of Murphy's. Outside in the main road the Mercedes-Benzes of these men waited to be re-entered. On the curled coatstand in the corner their full-length Antartex sheepskin coats hung. They wore square rings of gold and bracelets whose links looked as if they might be useful in a fight. Hard shrewd faces crested their big bodies. They were off the rigs, in Lillie Langtry's to get in the mood before a night onshore with the dalls and the drink. They had the stilted gentleness of athletes. It made them the nearest thing to heroes the evening could offer, in a place making so high a bid for atmosphere as Langtry's, with its purple plush and brass lamps and oldness slapped on over the same new underneath as anywhere else.

Elise looked at the burned sweetcorn, not even took off the husk, that Craig had ordered. He'd changed in America, right enough. Perhaps there were a lot of things new about him now. Loving someone was like that. New things happened to them and it was a new thing for you too. Bringing you together, in a sense. She wondered, even if she did go to America, if she could ever fancy a whole green pepper scared out of its wits like that, looking like a frog's got stepped on.

Her Diet Lilt came in a tall glass with a line at the top to control spurts of generosity on the part of the bar staff. The line came off if you scratched it with a knife, not if you did so with a fingernail. She didn't want to find these things out but Craig was making all this silence, and she had to do something. In their own home there'd be things to do if he took silent, but out like this, now, it was harder. Plus, she was shy of the pitta bread. Would you eat it like a carry-out or, being here, use the knife and fork provided since the two of them were sitting down not walking along or snogging in between mouthfuls?

She preferred a reunion by the sea or at the chippy, always had. It took them back to their beginning. She never had to bother then with the people they'd become on top of the ones they recognized at once in each other: efficient Elise who remembered her calculator and Craig who'd not and needed one for his maths exam so he'd took it off her and brought her for a cod roe fry with pineapple fritters to follow after school. They ate walking along the sea edge, the food and, it seemed, the air, hot and crisp and sweet and salt in their mouths and hair, with the smell of iron and fish and ships coming down damp with the night.

'It's a calculator works by the sun's rays,' said Elise, for something to say, because Craig was that old, sixteen, and she thought it might be greedy to pass comment on the fritters. Her fingers were grease to the bone, and there was salt in her papercuts and sugar in her bunches. It was brilliant, but she'd no idea what to say to her mother when she got in late that night.

'Just tell her you've been to America,' said Craig, but he took her home good as gold and explained about the calculator and the examination and the obligation he'd felt to give Elise a wee something to say thanks. After that he was in her house most days. Her parents bought him a calculator for his seventeenth birthday. She began to worry they'd put him off by being keen. He showed no sign of this however, and seemed to like being asked to do the things a son does, but for her parents, not his own, who were busy with their garden pond and fixture concession. They travelled sometimes, for the sculptures, that arrived twice a year in a big lorry, wrapped in blankets, looking like a grey extended family arriving at hospital, complete with pets.

Craig cleaned her parents' old lawnmower, even though his own mum and dad had a Hayter Hovercut, on summer sabbaths, easing its tired blades and joints with 1001 oil, before pouring the bin of fine clippings into the compost tip. Before going home on a Wednesday night, if he'd been over to her house, he'd save her mother and put out the dustbin, a drum of hefty pale shineless metal, ribbed like something military. She'd kiss him after that and be at once interested and bored by the possibilities that lay in so adult a routine so early in her life. It seemed dignified and glamorous to be kissing someone who knew that her mother disinfected and dried the bin on a Thursday, someone who now smelled of the peelings and papers in that bin. It was exciting to imagine being with Craig so long that she knew everything about him. The feeling that they were both old and young was good. The being old was a fantasy like being beautiful or dying, things that could never happen.

Never did she feel that she had leapfrogged something she might miss, for she saw her friends who went from boy to boy looking old and messed, like babies too late for bed.

Positioned about Lillie Langtry's at certain points where no real, weighty human might rest were life-size rag dolls dressed in Edwardian clothes. Lillie herself sat on top of the liqueurs section, legs crossed and diamanté-buckled shoes hanging too loosely to be coquettish in front of the yellow and blue and green drinks in their mad scientist's bottles. At the back of the bottles was a mirror, so you saw double the drink. The rag figures were stuffed with kapok, soft lumpy stuff that they very slowly shed through their loose lock-knit bodies, so that there lay about each floppy figure, after a time in the one pose, a faint sheepish shadow. The faces of these big dolls were stiff, flat and starchy. Nostrils, lashes, dimples and brows were achieved by stitching. The hands of the dolls were like seals' flippers, the fingers inseparable.

As time passed at Lillie Langtry's each evening, the dolls, that had begun the evening seeming to have little to do with the actual appearance and bearing of humans, seemed to grow more real, as the drinkers and diners, courting couples and spouses, sacrificed their individuality to the softening forces available at the bar or in one another's company, or bestowed by the advance of night. The dolls remained unchanged, slumped, inward-looking, but not so inhuman as they had appeared, simply preoccupied.

By the morning they had become empty again. It was part of the interest of going to Lillie Langtry's to see where the staff would reposition the dolls next. Although to move the dolls was the prerogative of the staff at the restaurant,

Craig had a friend Murdo who'd been sacked from his position on the garnish and maintenance side for posing two of the dolls in a way that was felt not to be tasteful or even historically accurate. It was true the dolls had a reserved look about them that made it hard to think of them taking anything like the kind of initiative Murdo had in mind.

Elise forked the mince out of her pitta, mashed it around in a swarfy tangle of raw carrot and swallowed it with a go of the Lilt. There were women arriving for the riggers now, great-looking girls on heels, carrying backwards off a few casual fingers short jackets with fur at the neck. Drinks arrived, ice, and small bottles of tonic. Coral nails flashed as the women palmed their nylons smooth over their insteps and up over ankle bracelets. Only a woman who couldn't groom herself like these ones would put the ankle bracelet on over the stockings, Elise had noticed. These women wore the bracelets like wedding rings, seriously, to say something about themselves.

Although it seemed that the women who had just arrived hardly spoke, the noise from the group of riggers grew. The men seemed to fill out, their voices too, in the presence of the women. The women looked in small mirrors at parts of themselves, eyeteeth, frown lines, upper lips, glimpses of throat. When they had put their mirrors away with snappings and zippings and wary lumbar movements of roosting, they started to try to get a view of parts of themselves harder to see, shoulder blades and elbows, knee-backs and the inner surfaces of nail ends; some looked at the tips of their high heels as though checking that nothing had been impaled there since the last look. One or two of the women spoke to one another to enlist help in checking some part of the construction that was hard to see by even the utmost craning – the hang of a dress over a buttock, the alignment of a belt with a hem at the back. It all looked private, but public, as though the women knew what gestures pleased the men, suggesting to them things about which they had been thinking for weeks out in the North Sea but could not name here or now.

Lillie Langtry watched with unsighted approval. Elise looked on and wondered where you learned those things. Was it from men or from other women, or was it born in you like knowing how to walk in heels and never telling people you'd heard their story before, and being unpopular with dogs?

Craig had returned to their table with his next lager. He'd filled out in America. He'd been that busy he probably had no time to eat right, just grab strange things. He'd not even had the time to be in touch with her, though he'd thought of her, he said, and here was the woollen jacket to prove it. A nice cut, with room for growth, she noticed; a jacket for the future, for when she'd a trout in her well. She thought of the old words he'd always used for the time when they would start a family, and knew herself lucky to be so young and with an unbroken past, shared with a man she knew so well she knew his way of using words. Right enough.

She smiled to herself in a way of which he had always been fond. It irked him now because it was the smile that told him she was happy. A trout in the well, Elise was thinking. Then after it's born, it's let loose in the stream.

Craig's gift to Elise was some kind of jacket for playing sports in, very American. It was made in China, she'd seen on the label that said 'ALL AMERICAN SPOTSGEAR'. It was a nice shade of grey, with big numbers on it in purple. It'd be good for walking Bonnie, her Airedale cross, before anyone got up and before Elise changed for work at the library.

No one noticed what you wore at the library, Craig said,

which made Elise take more care than ever. There were people came in there saw no one but the library staff from year's end to year's end. Why should they think the whole world lived in stained flannel and clotted wool?

Craig had been watching the women with the riggers while he stood at the bar looking as though he were deciding what vintage of Tennants to ask for. If you were with someone from the age of sixteen it was natural to look at women, thought Elise, and these women were for looking at. He'd've been half the man if he'd not keeked.

None the less, Craig returned to their table looking as though he expected her to start in on him about it. Had he not noticed she never did?

Craig was fidgety. One of the women in the group was getting under his skin. It was a bother that she kept looking at him. How was he supposed to jilt Elise with that slatch looking on? She was a redhead with the skin of a brunette and a suit all bobbles in lilac, chained over the bosoms. It was her drink told Craig why she bothered him. She was drinking a schooner of something that was lilac too. It was Parfait Amour, that looks like meths but moves slower out the bottle, held back by the sugar. There's been a fuss at the Lonnachs and Creel bar of the inn on Loch Lomondside when that liquor had been called for by a handsome woman with a high-spending oilman fresh in from Texas to Glasgow. Craig'd had to cycle over to the stores at Ardlui and there was no Perfect Armour there. They tracked it down at the minister's house; the bottle had been a gift from his son-in-law who worked for human rights somewhere they didn't have them and got queer gear duty-free. It had been this very redhead had wanted that purple drink he'd cycled for, Craig was sure. It stood to reason. She'd a right nerve to be here too, that one.

Elise watched Craig scrape the black off of a courgette on his dish. He hated the skin, so he just ate the part of the veg that remained between the charred part and the skin. It was mostly seeds, which he picked out of his teeth with one of the cardboard Lillie Langtry's matches that got soggy very quick. There was a little pain behind her heart as she thought that he wasn't enjoying his food this evening. She felt for him like that, in the anxious everyday way. When they were married, she'd help him with everything so he needn't end up an evening out full of charcoal and compost even if ate off of an oval plate with dishwasherproof lilies painted on. They could choose things together then.

'I'll just off and get myself a poke of scratchings,' she said, and walked over to the bar. Closer to the group of laughing men and preening women, she smelled the burst and fallen smell of big flowers that was the mixed perfumes of the women, and saw that the men were having floppy steaks, from which the women were cutting wee ribbons that they ate off forks as if the meat were pasta.

The redheaded woman in her suit that was like bunched lilacs saw Elise and envied her, independent, neat, fresh, and able to buy herself a pack of snacks any time and eat it. She raised her half-full purple glass to Elise and smiled with her cheeks at her over it. Her smile said, '*Men.*'

Elise smiled back. Her smile had no words behind it because she had no answer to the comment in the plural.

'You're very free with your foolish grins,' said Craig, as she opened the scratchings, did not take one and put them in front of him.

'She's nice. She smiled. Nice to see a person smile here at a stranger.'

'You'll be getting plenty smiling in the library, no?'

'It's quieter.'

'Smiles don't make sound do they, Elise? Eh?'

'There are no ladies in purple raising their glasses to me in Reference, Craig.'

Here they were using their names against each other on this night when she wanted to please him and he wanted to hurt her in the least noticeable way.

It was she who unfroze first.

'Will we have a sweet? You'll've had great sweets in the States.' The moment she had spoken she heard her foolish eagerness.

'Aye, the usual things.' He finished the most recent lager. 'There was Mississippi Mud Pie, Key Lime Pie, your Banana Toffee Pie. The usual things. Pies.'

Elise said nothing. She looked down at the Lillie Langtry's menu where these very puddings, described in shocking detail, were listed. She decided to pursue her curiosity. If he was this bored, or that out of it, he wouldn't notice.

'There'll've been lovely women over there.'

'Och, gorgeous,' said Craig, bitterly. 'Gorgeous.' He might just have received a bill for the gas. In his mind there paraded the beauties of the kitchen on Loch Lomondside, three married women and a wee wanting girl who peeled potatoes all to the same size and said she ate the peelings at home at the hostel in the evenings.

This was dreadful. He was wanting to tell Elise the truth.

He looked over to the purple woman. She was starting on another of her drinks. She gave him a very familiar look, not flirtatious, but reproving. The cheeky besom, who was she to give him a ticking off? He finished the scratchings, and told the waitress he'd have an Irish coffee with the sweet, and another lager just for now.

A pretty woman sitting for some reason above the racks of bottles looked kindly at Craig. She understood him.

Then he realized his mistake, and looked away from the Lillie Langtry doll as though it'd seen through to his own stuffing.

Elise asked for a cup of tea, which was moody of her, he thought. For relief from her familiarity and from her clean parting and nice teeth, he looked at the purple lady, who had put down her drink now and was smoking. Through the smoke he saw her face, and it knew him and knew what was in his mind. This painted woman was judging him through her filthy smoke.

He'd a good mind right enough to go over to her and tell her what a troublemaker she was wherever she went with her Parfait Amour and legs and eyes. No, first he must be cruel to be kind and make Elise see there was no big day ahead, just the usual small ones.

'Elise, while I was in, eh, America I did, em, a lorra thinking. I thought a lot. Know what I mean?'

'Uh huh,' said Elise, looking forward to her tea and wondering how she could get Craig to let her drive without upsetting him. When he used to say 'lorra' he was either drunk or trying to impress someone. But now it was maybe an American accent.

This American thinking had been effortful, she saw. And, that tired with the trip over from the States, he wasn't sober, either.

'Thinking, aye, right enough. In America.' He saw himself, thinking in America, in his mind. Since they were taking place in America these thoughts were unusually pure and free and big, with enormous cactuses and skyscrapers surrounding them. Everything was important in America. Those American thoughts of his were very important.

'I'm just away to the toilet for a moment,' said Elise. 'I'll not be long. It's magic to see you again. You've not being looking after yourself, though.'

Craig's American thoughts receded. The cactuses disappeared behind the rainy hills of Loch Lomond, the skyscrapers fell like settling smoke. He thought of the deadly afternoon in the coach travelling back up, the video history of the clans playing on the screen at the front and the way the old people didn't emerge from the chemical toilet for half an hour at a time.

He'd have one more try, before his habits closed around him and the old familiar things had won over the shiny new stuff he just knew must be waiting somewhere for him.

'It's just we were that young when we started, Ella. I just need a space.' Aye, that was it, space was the word he'd been guddling for. 'The space, Ella, I need it. To myself. See, you crowd me. I'm crowded. Stop crowding me.' Will I never stop saying that? he thought. Let's try another angle.

'Just give me space,' he concluded. Though all he could think of was a locked box without windows being took round corners he couldn't see at a terrible rate while he listened to the past going round and round on a tape and his own dirt swilled around below him. 'It's a bit of space that I need. Just so's I can see where I'm going. God, Ella, I don't even know where I've been.' In warming to his subject, he was blowing it away.

She'd seen at once what he was saying. It was lucky she was on the way to the washroom, any road.

The ladies had a woman in a picture hat in silhouette on the door. Inside was a wee sofa with another of those daft dolls sitting on it. From the safety of the cubicle Elise let herself go and talked to it loudly to keep herself from crying.

'Space. He needs space. It's space he needs right enough. I crowd him out. See that, I crowd him out. We were that young when we began we need to go into *space.*'

Elise felt better as she came out. The lilac woman was waiting on the sofa beside the doll, looking unsurprised.

'Whoever spouted all that blash at you must've been in America, my wee peat,' she said. 'It'll pass over, right enough. Water under the bridge, I'd call it.'

GOODBYE,
ROBBIE TUESDAY...

Chris Roberts

After many false summits, we finally reached the top of
the hill. The icy wind blowing in from the river whipped
wildly around us and almost pushed me off balance. I was
still wearing my good new shoes from the funeral and the
grips weren't worth anything. Jamie took my hand and
led me around the hillside, leaning in to the slope until
he found a hollow place, smooth and level like a shelf,
and with gorse bushes all around for a windbreak. Stroked
by the wind every day, the bushes were bent about double
but still growing, their knuckled roots clinging on to the
scrubby hillside.

Jamie shoved me forward into the hollow and flopped
down beside me. It was so quiet out of the wind. I felt
exhausted, but kind of thrilled all the same. This seemed
a safe place. I looked up at Jamie, feeling the heat in my
blood from the overworked engine of my heart and lungs.
We grinned at each other.

'Made it,' Jamie said.

I nodded. 'Can we eat now?' I asked him. 'I'm starving
after all that exercise.'

'Robbie, we've just started. How're we gonna get away
if you've got to feed your face every five minutes?'

I felt myself blushing, but I could see Jamie was tempted
too. He kept shooting quick glances at his school satchel,

knowing it was filled with all kinds of goodies he'd pinched from the house after we slipped away from the hotel. It was strange seeing him dressed in his school clothes, with his black armband still on and his hair all neat. We had ditched our new black ties back at the house, but hadn't risked getting caught by taking the time to change our clothes.

After a few seconds' thought he gave in and started to unbuckle the leather straps of the schoolbag. I sat up, watching him with that admiration that only wee brothers feel. Jamie was ten and I was six. Six and a half, now I think of it. The half seemed to count for an awful lot back then.

He got the schoolbag open and reached inside. I was already slavering like a bulldog and shifting about on my knees in anticipation as he brought the contents out one by one and laid them on the ground. A tin of Heinz tomato soup. Two big KitKats. One of those huge squares of Scotbloc cooking chocolate. A tin of Campbell's meat-balls in onion gravy. A bar of Lifebuoy soap. The blue transistor radio he got for his birthday. And a small ball of string. Then the bag was empty.

'Is that it?' I asked.

Jamie looked up at me through his dark fringe.

'What's wrong wi' it?'

'Isn't there anything to drink?'

He sighed with impatience. 'Robbie, for God's sake. This is the outdoors. *Last of the Mohicans* and that. You never saw Hawkeye asking Chingachgook, "Where's that bottle of skoosh?" Well did you?'

I shook my head.

'We'll find water,' Jamie continued. 'We'll drink and wash in clear running rivers with the deer and the crea-tures of the wild.'

That was him away. Jamie was always like that.

'What about *now*?' I demanded, stretching the last word as far as it would go to make sure he understood the thirst I had on me.

He threw up his hands in helplessness. 'Look, that's all I could carry, see?' he said. 'Here, have a bit of this.' He tore open the Cellophane around the Scotbloc and broke off four big chunks for me and the same for himself. I bit into it and felt better immediately. I liked all kinds of chocolate, but cooking chocolate was the best, as long as you didn't get caught stealing it out the baking cupboard. Good Boy buttons for dogs were nice too. My pal Andy and me shared a whole big tub once with Andy's dog, Jasper, then we both pretended to be dogs, except Jasper who just sat and watched us like we were crazy. I laughed so much I peed myself.

Jamie fiddled with the wee radio and it crackled into life. A song we both really liked was just starting, 'Ruby Tuesday' by the Rolling Stones.

> She would never say where she came from
> Yesterday don't matter if it's gone.

The music somehow brought us back together and we both grinned through chocolate teeth. The Stones were Mum's favourite. She had been playing the radio in the kitchen one time when Jamie had said to me, 'That's what I'm calling you from now on. Robbie Tuesday.' And that was that. Once Jamie's mind was decided you couldn't shift it. Robbie Tuesday. I thought it was just about the coolest name I had ever heard. It beat seven colours of shite out of MacLeod, that was for sure. And it really was my favourite song too. Apart from 'Chim Chim Cheree' from *Mary Poppins.*

We didn't say anything for a minute or two. Jamie was opening up his Swiss army knife with sixteen blades, scissors, bottle- and tin-openers and things. I looked out over the green and yellow gorse bushes and back down the hill to see how far we had come. You could see the whole town from up there, long and thin, clinging to the shore like the great, broad river was the mystical source of all life itself. Which it was, of course. The cranes of the shipyards stood up tall and strong like sentries keeping watch over all the factories and houses. It was really impressive from the hill, like you could see the sense of it. Down among the streets there didn't seem to be any sense to anything. I remembered a question I wanted answered.

'Jamie, why did you say that to Mr Fisher?'

Jamie shrugged. 'It's the truth,' he said and then he was quiet again. He had a way about him of letting you know when you shouldn't ask any more.

I rolled on to my back and looked up into the afternoon sky, listening to the song, smelling the air. There were lots of grey, wispy clouds being chased away by big black ones from across the river. Rain coming.

> When you change with every new day,
> Still I'm gonna miss you.

I liked it there, feeling the grass on my back, looking up into the sky. Too much had been happening too quickly in the past few days. Now everything was happening somewhere else, to other people, and I felt safe.

The sky was amazing. Right from when I was dead wee, I used to go out into the garden and lie on my back, looking up. Jamie had told me about the world being round, but I knew that was just one of his stories. I told him: if it was round, you'd fall off. Sometimes he really acted like my head zipped up the back. Sure enough though, he showed me where it was written in a book and the thought of it made my head spin.

I lay like that until I got the feeling that actually I wasn't looking up at all. I was stuck on a kind of ceiling and any moment the glue or whatever it was that was holding me on would give way and I was going to fall into the swirling cloud and fall and fall for ever. I closed my eyes just as the song finished. Jamie snapped the radio off and started to clear everything into his bag.

'Best be off,' he said.

I kept my eyes shut and lay still. Suddenly things were happening again, but I didn't want anything to happen. I wanted things to be back the way they had been before, or else just stop and let me catch up.

'Come on.' Jamie was getting insistent. I heard him buckling the schoolbag shut.

'I can't,' I told him. And I really felt that I couldn't. It was all I could do to speak.

'You've got to, Robbie. I told you, we'll be fine. I'll build a shelter and we can catch rabbits and fish and that. We'll take tatties from the fields and steal eggs out the hen-houses. There's roots and berries you can eat, you'll see.'

He was away again, but he just didn't get it. I wasn't worried about us, I was worried about Mum.

'Who's gonna look after her?' I said.

'What? Who?'

'Who'll look after Mum when we're gone?' I pushed myself up on my elbows and opened my eyes to let him see I meant it. My hands knotted themselves into fists as I stood up to face him. I shouted in his face, 'Who'll look after her?'

Jamie looked astonished. I could see he had never thought of that. He sat down again and told me to do the same. 'Let's just wait a minute,' he said. 'Give us a bit of peace to think.'

I was ahead of him there. My mind was already replaying everything that had happened. It was still only five days since Thursday morning. There were some things that, when they changed, changed faster than you could have believed, and then they stayed changed too. That was the worst part.

I had known something was up as soon as I woke. For one thing, I woke myself. Nobody had to pull the covers off me and force me to open my eyes and get moving. And Jamie's bed was empty, which was strange too, because he didn't usually get up without saying anything. I could hear voices, very quiet, and see daylight through the curtains. I remember thinking that maybe Mum and Dad had just forgotten about me and if I didn't make any noise they wouldn't remember until it was halfway through the morning and there'd be no point in going to school until after lunch. I reached under my bed and got out my *Popeye* comic, very carefully, so as not to alert anyone to my presence. Then I lay on my stomach with the comic spread open on the pillow.

They'd had that big argument the night before. These days it seemed like they were always arguing. I remember once Dad had hit Mum, blacked her eye, and she'd told us she was going to leave him. She even went to see a lawyer but in the end she stayed because of me being small. That was what Jamie said.

I didn't know what they were arguing about that night, and neither did Jamie. It was one of the big ones though. Lots of slamming and shouting and Dad swearing at the top of his voice. I pulled the covers over my head and tried to force myself to sleep but the noise was too frightening. Then things would quieten down for a while and that was worse because you wanted so much for it to be over but you could never be sure it wasn't just about to flare up again.

I heard the living-room door open and recognized

Dad's footsteps stomping down the hall and past our room. The front door opened and quickly slammed shut and then I heard Mum go and click the latch, locking him out. I listened as she walked back into the living room and closed the door again. There were a couple of seconds' silence, before this really loud music started up. Mum's Verdi, the one she played to soothe herself, she said. It stopped with a sudden crackle and I knew she'd put the headphones on. I didn't say anything and neither did Jamie. In ten seconds I had fallen asleep.

Being Popeye must be brilliant, I thought. Just able to burst open a can of spinach, then wham! All your problems solved. I was imagining myself stopping Mum and Dad fighting just by knocking their heads together and telling them to behave or there was plenty more where that came from when Jamie came in, wearing his jeans and patterned shirt, not his school clothes, and sat down on his bed across from me. He clasped his hands and stared at his shoes for a bit, before looking up. His face was white, eyes hollow.

'Dad's dead,' he told me.

I nearly laughed. Not because it was funny, it just sort of happened. But I stopped myself. I could see Jamie was serious. I asked him what had happened and he started to cry. He wrapped his arms across his chest and threw himself back on the bed, curled up like a baby. I had never seen Jamie blub like that before and I couldn't understand it. He'd always said he hated Dad.

Things got really confused then. I remember wanting to cry, or feeling that I should, but there was nothing there. Mum came in and took me under one arm and reached for Jamie with the other. He fought her off at first and then started sobbing into her side. She held us really close and the three of us stayed like that for a while. Mum wasn't crying either, which made me feel better, but her eyes were hollow, same as Jamie's.

Later on, people started coming round and for the next couple of days there were lots of phone calls and visits from family and neighbours and friends and people I had never seen before as Mum got everything organized for the funeral. It was all a bit unreal, that time. Gran came over and cooked our meals and helped Mum with things. Jamie and I kept going to school and were sent out to play after, like our lives were just supposed to continue untouched.

The other kids at school were alright. I don't know if the teacher had told them to be nice to us, but mostly I remember them simply keeping their distance and being really gentle and respectful. The exception was Don Wilkie.

Months before, Dad had given Don Wilkie a sore ear for throwing stones or something. It was the first time I had heard a grown-up calling anyone a toerag. After Dad died, Don would do things like banging into me really hard and acting like it was an accident, or else if he was with his mates, he would pretend to clear his throat, but really he was saying 'Yer Dad's dead,' right in my ear and trying to disguise it as a cough.

I was coming home after school one day when Don ran up behind me and grabbed my bag off my shoulder. He was making faces and calling me names, whirling the bag over his head like he was going to chuck it over somebody's wall, when suddenly he started to howl because Jamie had shot him right in the eye from a water pistol filled with vinegar. He put his hands up to his face and ran off and Jamie and I did the same.

Don's Mum came round later on but Mum wouldn't let her in, so she stood in the porch shouting how we'd blinded her little boy. Jamie and I lay behind the couch giggling like anything. He had keeked out the window and said Don's eye was all red and raised up like a boil. He was a right bastard, Don Wilkie. His mother had no idea. Anyway, the eye got better in a few days.

But now, there she was outside the front door calling Mum for everything. And that was how we heard a bit more of what had happened. In between all the cursing and threats we got some of the story of Dad dying. The rest we pieced together from people who would talk and forget we were in the room.

Mum had told us it was his heart and that was right enough. What she didn't say was that she was the one who had found his body in the morning, sitting behind the wheel of the car, with his coat on like he was about to drive off to work. He must have left the house after their argument, opened up the garage, got into the car and been hit by the heart attack right away. Neighbours and people walking in the street said they had heard a car horn going, several short blasts and then a great long one before it stopped, but nobody had known where it was coming from. I must have been asleep because I couldn't remember hearing anything. And Mum told Gran how she kept seeing like in a film this picture of herself with her headphones on, sitting in the living room, tense as a knife, she said, trying to stop her tears, with the opera that she loved and Dad hated smothering all the thoughts in her mind while through the wall her husband was dying, clawing the air in desperation, pounding the car horn for attention, for the rescuer who would never arrive because she could not hear him.

They cremated the body, so there was none of that throwing dirt onto the coffin like in the films. We stood in a line, Mum and Jamie and me and shook hands with people who said they were sorry to Mum and told us we had to be brave young soldiers.

It was at the hotel afterwards that the thing happened with Mr Fisher. I don't remember when we first met Mr Fisher, but he was always Mum's friend and not Dad's. Sometimes his name would fly about during their fights. I liked Mr Fisher. He was always very smartly dressed and smelled of nice things. Old Spice aftershave and Vitalis hair lotion. He had a big old Volvo car he said was made of battleship steel and which was all polished wood and red leather inside.

In the days after Dad died, Mr Fisher came to the house a lot. Mum said he was a great help, but I heard Gran say that she didn't think it was right and that people would get the wrong idea if Mum wasn't careful. Mum said she had more important things to worry about than what people thought.

The hotel was really posh, meaning the waiters and everybody were all stiff and formal and the room was freezing. There was a nice smell from the food though, big plates on top of white linen tablecloths. Jamie went and got some sandwiches and hot sausage rolls to warm us up. There were a lot of people there, but we were the only children and nobody paid us any attention until Mr Fisher came over and sat down.

'Nice grub, boys?' he said, smiling. He had very white teeth. He held out an arm and without thinking I let him pick me up and sit me on his lap, folding me into his welcoming atmosphere of male scents. Jamie stayed where he was.

'Have you ever been to a football match, lads?' Mr Fisher asked. I shook my head. Jamie was quiet.

'How would you like to see a game with your Uncle Davie?'

Nobody had ever called Mr Fisher Uncle Davie, certainly not Jamie or me. I was trying to think who he meant when I heard Jamie say something under his breath.

'What was that, James?'

Jamie stood right in front of him, fists clenched, eyes like fire. I wriggled to get free, but Mr Fisher's arm gripped me. I saw Jamie stick his chin out like he did before a fight.

'I said I know *your* game. You're after our mum, you dirty big bastard!'

The whole room went dead quiet. Jamie had fairly shouted. God knows where Mum came from but suddenly she was there and the back of her hand walloped Jamie in the face, knocking him into the table, sandwiches flying. Mr Fisher stood up, and I was off his lap and out of the way fast. He was spreading his hands out as if about to say the boy didn't mean it or some such line when Mum balled her ring hand up into a tight little fist, screamed an obscenity and let him have it square across the lips.

Mr Fisher sat down and everyone in the room kind of froze. He moved his tongue around inside his mouth, feeling for damage. For a moment I thought he was going to spit his teeth out one by one like in the cartoons. Instead he got to his feet and said, very calmly, 'Please accept my most sincere condolences.' Then he gave Mum a little bow from the neck and walked out of the hotel, and out of our lives for ever. He walked very erect and with tremendous dignity, even when he skited slightly on a wee bit of egg mayonnaise on the floor. Please accept my most sincere condolences. He was alright, Mr Fisher. But Mum was outstanding.

'Fuck off!'

Smash!

Brilliant.

* * *

35

In our nest on the hillside, I rolled over and looked at Jamie. He had stood up and was looking at the sky, at the clouds sweeping in from the river. You could smell the coming rain in the air. Jamie seemed very far away, but he must have known I was looking at him, because without turning round he said: 'I heard it, Robbie.'

I thought he meant something on the hill, an animal maybe, and I stood up quickly.

'What is it?'

'I heard Dad,' he said softly. 'I was awake. I heard the car horn. I knew it was him. I knew there must be trouble. But I didn't do anything.'

The rain began falling and the wind got up at the same time. Jamie raised his voice to be heard.

'I knew something was wrong, Robbie. I mean, I think I knew he would die unless I helped him. But I didn't go. I pulled the covers over my head and pretended I was sleeping. I killed him, Robbie.'

'No, Jamie. It was his heart. Mum said. The doctor, everybody said.'

'Aye, I did. I killed him.' Crying now, leaning over the edge like he was going to take off.

'Nobody killed him, he just died.'

'But I *wanted* him to die,' Jamie howled. 'I wished him dead. That's how I killed him.' He looked back at me. 'Ach, you're too wee to understand.'

He knew it always got me livid when he said that. 'I'll show you who's too wee,' I yelled. I flew at him, but he spun around much too fast. The packed schoolbag caught me in the chest and sent me sprawling. Then Jamie plunged through the curtain of rain and he was off down the hillside, leaping, flying. I scrambled after him, a little winded, but determined to catch up and make him take back what he'd said.

We fairly bombed it down the hill, rain blasting right

in our faces. I was running so fast my feet hardly touched the ground. When I got back to the dyke next to the road where the first houses were, Jamie was waiting and he was Jamie again. Big smile, big brother. I bent over with my hands on my knees to catch my breath.

'I won't tell, Jamie, honest,' I told him. He handed me another bit of chocolate.

'Race you home!' he said, and tore off down the street, only this time he let me catch him up.

We ran home side by side, rain in rivers on our hair and skin, our good clothes soaked through. As we ran I tried to remember the way the town had looked from up on the hill, when everything seemed to be there for a reason, but the picture had faded from my mind.

We had just let ourselves into the house when the front door opened again and Gran came in, leading Mum and half a dozen worried-looking relations.

'You see,' Gran said, pointing at the two of us. 'I told you they'd be here.' And she started telling us off, but Mum pushed past her and grabbed hold of us, falling to her knees and pulling Jamie down with her. I was still standing. It was strange, at six, being eyelevel to other people. We hugged tight for a long, long time. Then Mum relaxed and sat back, still with her arms around us both.

'Three musketeers,' she said.

Jamie rolled his eyes at me, meaning just humour her, but I felt that I knew what she meant and I remember thinking that this was the end of it now, that the grieving part was over and, if it was going to be just the three of us together from now on, that was alright with me.

TEUCHTER DANCING WHEN THE LIGHTS GO OUT

Raymond Soltysek

My left hand switched off last night.

Something inside me broke the connection and the nerves went dead. Just like that, out like a light. One millisecond, electrical pulses course along neural pathways. The next, gone, cold, defunct, and the whole thing's ready for the scrap yard.

I had a glass in my hand at the time. It dropped, bouncing off the padded arm of the chair, sending the cat beelining under the sofa. Just as well it was a vodka, not a cup of coffee to scald my legs. Not that they would feel it. They switched off months ago.

Allison came in, asked me if I was all right. I said yeah, just clumsy. I didn't tell her, seemed no point. She wiped up the puddle. I said she looked tired – fucking platitude – and she said yes she was. She asked me if I needed anything, I said a body transplant, and she smiled and kissed me good night, her lips dry against my cheek. She tidied up in the kitchen, opening and closing cupboards a few times. The kettle was boiled for her hot chocolate, the cat's litter tray was shaken. Then she went to bed.

I sat there and studied the switched-off hand. It looked no different, knuckles bulging, wrinkles, fine hairs. The nails were bitten badly, a lifelong habit I'll finally break if I can't get my bloody fingers near my mouth. Every cloud, they say.

I turned it over with my right. Soft hands. No manual work and lousy at DIY. Pink fingerprints. Long life line. Very long life line. Bastard.

Left hands are useless things anyway. Can't write love letters with them, or bowl a yorker, or toss yourself off in the middle of the night reading a porno mag from your secret store. They fight against learning to juggle, sulk awkwardly when meeting somebody new. Fucking hopeless, they are.

This is how I do it, since the rage left. The part of me I lose, the part which switches off, is made redundant. Always was superfluous. Never really needed that bit, did I, darling? The legs were fine: gawky extremities which wore out expensive shoes, and the left one (left ones again, note) was crap at football. The prick was a bit trickier, though. Its use had to be redefined. Now, it's a convenient bit of pipework to connect to the plastic bag that fills at my side during the day.

Wasn't always like that, of course. In the beginning, we gave our genitals nicknames, they spoke to each other in silly voices and then we'd laugh at our childishness. She always made me feel good. Sometimes wonderful.

Like that weekend, a crisp New Year when we said *let's do something different* and we lorded it up at some laird's long-pawned castle. There were claymores on the wall of the banquet hall, and round shields with those wee peaks in the middle like seventeenth-century Gaultier bras, built for the big, big women of the North. Settees of every period, every style, floral, gold filigree, brown Dralon. Mantel shelves piled with stuff, antique candlesticks beside plastic snowstorms of Buckingham Palace and a gold 1960s James Bond DB5 complete with working ejector seat and bulletproof shield. Owning a stately home's easy, just never, ever throw anything away, it's bound to become a collector's item. And I had two of those Aston Martins, and a fucking Batmobile.

The ceilidh band had an accordionist the women dropped dead for and a drummer who wore a tartan nightshirt and had red hair halfway down his back and a definite fancy for Allison. They pummelled their music out, and the wee violinist in the short black skirt whirled round and round and stamped her feet and her thighs made all the men shudder and toast her with the whisky, flowing amber, warm, reddening noses and making belches peppery. As much was spilled between clinking glasses as was drunk, and the kisses were deep and aromatic.

The floor was ace, shining abalone, perfect for dancing. Oh fuck, the dancing. We were wild with it, charging up and down, in and out, under arms and over skipping feet, stripping the willow and dashing the sergeant. The pounding of a stitch, breathlessly working it off again, the feel of a waist, spun round the inside of the forearm, lost, whirling off to another grip, replaced, tight, hard, slim waists, eager to be held, desperate to be released. Allison laughed, shone so perfect-cheekboned, flirted maniacally and always found her way back to me, and we leaned our foreheads together and mingled sweat turning rapidly cold in the lank bits of hair we flicked from our eyes. We collapsed against each other, wheezed halfway off the dance floor until the band struck up and one of us said *Oh yeah! I know how to do this*, and turned to begin again and again. We'd be called into an eightsome, arms arcing us over, *join us, join us*, and off we'd go, and I couldn't help directing traffic. *I'm a teacher, veteran of social dancing*, I'd say, *Ah-heel, toe, heel, toe, one-two-three turn*, and Allison would laugh and do it wrong deliberately, *no, no, round*

THAT way, and I'd realize the fun all lay in fucking it up, reeling about in a rabble of skirt and shoe and twisting heads.

'Til three we went on, and made lifelong friends we never saw again, and the drummer got the message and toasted us and slapped me on the back. We all held conversations like running battles along the mahogany corridors, snipers popping heads out of doorways to fire jokes at us.

We went to our room and made love like athletes, getting embarrassed in mid flow by the squeaking bed, Allison flipping the mattress onto the floor with one superhuman finger and covering me with kisses. Her legs were over my shoulders when I came the deepest ever in her, and I watched myself laugh in the wardrobe mirror and I proposed to her then and there, even though we'd already been married for three years. She snaked her thighs around my waist and accepted and we lay for an hour and found the mattress five times as heavy when we put it back on the bed.

We left early in the morning, after top'n'tailing in a bath as big as a submarine pen, washing each other's toes and losing the soap just so I could look for it in the places that made her squeak. *This is the best*, we said, *the best*, and I don't think we were ever happier.

I heard Allison's bedroom door open, her footsteps slippered soft along the hallway. She stopped, perhaps on the point of coming in, her hand reaching out to the doorknob. Then she turned and went back. Let her sleep.

I've been told. Bit by bit I'll switch off. Left arm next, probably. Right hand, arm. Hearing. Sight. My bowels have been opened, and my tongue will be stopped.

But my brain won't. It'll reel on, disconnected from all the switched off fragments. Nothing listening to it. Nothing obeying it.

I'm ready for it, though. I know all the steps. Gay

Gordons. Strip the Willow. Canadian Barn Dance. Military Fucking Two-Step.

I'll be teuchter dancing.

PORKY PIG
AND FANDO FILLAMON

Andrew Greig

Fando Fillamon tripped Porky Pig neat as anything as they trailed into the class.

Stella saw Fando's tackity boot clip Porky's ankle then white legs tangle and blur as Porky skites into Dewar's desk. A pile of blue jotters topples, Porky is greiting with books skittering from his wide black-short arse onto the floor. She reaches out and catches the last one in mid-air: *Patrick Geddes, Primary 7.*

She can still feel the greasy roughness of that blue card cover.

Lying on the couch with her blue notebook, half-watching afternoon television, she smells a classroom in June thirty years back, scent of sweat and chalk and books and cut grass outside. And of course she sees Porky, and Fando as his thin wide mouth moves. She feels the tickle of sweat under her eleven-year-old armpits.

'Patterson! Are you in the furniture moving business, man? Get up!'

Fando winked at Stella.

'Nice catch,' he said.

Stella put the jotter on the desk, wouldn't look at him.

'Get up, Patterson!'

Porky obediently jerked up and his head hit the corner of the desk. Wood into bone, a crunch like no other. Standing beside Fando she saw how the water from Porky's eyes collected the drip from his nose, and how Fando's hands were curling as the class waited.

'He tripped me, sir!'

Dewar shook his head. His dark moustache flattened.

'Did you trip Patterson, Mister Fillamon?'

Fando looked straight at him.

'No.'

'No, *sir*.'

'No, sorr,' Fando said, broadening the Irish. 'Our feet got tangled as we came in the dorr. Sorr.'

Dewar looked down but Stella saw the side of his mouth twitch. As an incomer she had to watch signals to understand anything. Porky sniffed, Fando stood still and relaxed and ready to run.

'So what's your version, Henderson?'

The class, those hyenas, shifted. Porky looked at her with watery blue eyes. Fando's eyes were green today, he was the tallest boy in the class, exactly her height. They could have been kin. Outsiders. Incomers.

'Well? A tangle or a trip, Miss Henderson?'

She's sweating in her clumpy shoes and mum's cut-down print dress. With the eyes on her, she hears her mum telling her one thing and her dad the opposite.

She chose neither.

'It looked like a . . . tango, sir.'

'A *tango*?'

'Yes, sir, like they were trying to dance but Peter fell. Sir.'

Laughter from the thickies at the back. Dewar's hand brushed over his mouth then thumped onto the desk.

'Ach, away and sit down the lot of you.'

She sat beside Seona. Fando winked as he went past.

Seona passed her a sweetie under the desk, the first she'd
been offered since she'd arrived at the school. Porky snivelled in the corner but no one was interested now.

They got out their books and she sat for a while feeling
confused. You could tell the truth, or you could tell a lie.
But there was a third way.

She stared at her jotter and sucked the sweetie quietly.

You could make them laugh.

It was like finding a new way home.

He was sitting cross-legged in the shade under the hawthorn tree at the top of High Field, fiddling with something in his lap.

'Nicely done, colleen,' he said without looking up.

She stopped and looked down at him.

'My name's Stella,' she said. 'And it was mean to pick
on Porky when everyone does.'

He looked up.

'We call all pretty girls colleen.'

Nobody spoke to her like that. Except for her family
and now Seona, almost no one spoke to her at all. And
she wasn't pretty, she was skinny and scraggy and had
frizzy hair. Anyway she didn't particularly want to be a
girl.

He uncrossed his legs and leaned back against the trunk
and flicked his dark hair and stared at her.

'I know why you didn't tell,' he said.

She reached up and held a branch and leaned from
side to side.

'I still think it was dead mean,' she said.

He opened his hands. He had a knife, an odd white
knife with a thin blade. Under the tree things smelled
strong and sweet and sickly all at once.

'Imagine being fat and everyone picking on you all the
time.'

45

He took the knife by the tip of the blade. He held his arm up and squinted like he was going to draw her.

'Sure, it was a devilment, colleen,' he said.

Fando grinned very white teeth and drew his arm back. She stopped swaying and stood still under the tree in her red dress and the sun hot between her shoulder blades.

'My name's Stella,' she said.

His arm brushed quickly across his face and the knife was juddering in the fence post. She blinked but didn't move. Even in her dreams she'd never been feart of Fando Fillamon.

'But if they weren't picking on him, it would be on you or me, wouldn't it now?' He rolled over and plucked out the knife. 'And you know that's true.'

'They wouldn't dare pick on you.'

'Paddy? Pape? Tinky bum?' He spat. 'If there was enough of them they would.'

She wanted to spit like him.

'Is that a gypsy knife?'

He grinned, flexed his hand, and the thin blade disappeared.

'Na. You'd best be looking, then.'

She dropped her duffel bag and sat down beside him. He shifted away, just a little, and then she felt dizzy and full of herself.

She lifted the haft from his brown palm and examined it. The handle was white and cool, with two silver hoops and a black button at one end.

'It's a flick knife. Himself got it in Paris from a gangster.' She turned it over. Paris. Gangsters. Flick knife. 'The handle's ivory.'

'From elephants' tusks? Real ivory?' His eyes glittered as he nodded. 'How does it work?'

His fingers brushed her palm. The lines on the back of his hand were like veins on the underside of leaves. He wrapped the shaft in his long fingers then bent his wrist, pressed and the blade was pointing at her chest.

'Let me try.'

He rolled on his back and looked up at the sky through the leaves, still clutching the knife.

'Ah, well now,' he said.

She leaned over him. The knife was in his leafy hand. It was hot in the hollow under the tree, and inside her dress she felt herself full and buzzing like a summer swarm looking for a different home. She slowly drew the blade from his hand then rolled away with her prize.

Press the button, fold the blade. Bend the wrist, press, turn and click! Every time she did it she felt more confident and more swarming inside. It was like stroking yourself over and over.

He was lying on his side watching her.

'Strike upward and it's serious,' he said. 'If you just want to cut, strike down.'

She pictured Porky falling, greiting, his head hitting the desk.

'I don't want to hurt anybody,' she said.

'And why would you indeed?'

He reached out one hand towards her. She knew what would happen now. Kissing. Rolling around. Something.

But he took the knife back, slipped it in his pocket and stood up. She tugged her dress down over her knees.

'Can I come with you to the camp?'

'Na. Himself will be there.'

'My dad drinks with your dad.'

'He's the only one here who does.'

She shrugged.

'My dad drinks with anyone who'll listen to him.'

He giggled like a wee boy.

'Mine too. But he wudn't stand for it. We don't mix.'

He looked down, shrugged. 'Sorry, colleen.'

Then he disappeared down the path towards the river where the gypsy caravans were, and she took the short cut home through the cornfield which grew much higher then.

She slipped the window up and went out headfirst. The moon was pale like a silver dollar plant and the drainpipe was already damp on her hands.

She got her knees onto the window ledge, glanced down at the flowerbed where the square of light from the kitchen window made all the wallflowers yellow whatever colour they were really. She tightened her dressing gown, then without pausing to think about it stood up on the ledge, facing in. One hand squeezed behind the pipe and the other gripped the ivy.

She wasn't really scared of this, it just made it more interesting to pretend she was. Three steps sideways on the little sloping ledge as she clung to the ivy, then her foot was on the lead skews. She groped for the porch roof then pulled herself over, turned round and hunkered down and looked out.

She could hear the murmur of her parents' voices below and a jazz record playing. She looked down the garden and over the wall and down the dip where the trees and river and gypsies were. The voices rose. 'You just please yourself!' she heard, then her dad's giggling laughter that nearly always worked. Her mother said something else she didn't quite catch, then the clink of a glass and another giggle. She sat very still, then the window was pulled down and the voices were cut off.

She pulled the cigarette from the top pocket of the dressing gown. She ran it under her nose, all smooth and cool and white like the ivory knife. She jabbed and parried at the silver dollar moon with her cigarette, then stuck it in her mouth. She thought about Porky, the white of him falling.

She cautiously struck a match on the slates. The moon made a haze in the damp air over her, like a pale waterfall pouring down. She sucked in and blew out. She would live in a cave behind a waterfall and be wild and free and please herself. Only Fando could visit.

She smoked and thought about it, trying not to cough.

Then it was playtime on the last morning of their last day at the wee school.

She wandered across the playground, sipping warm thick milk through a straw. She felt a bit sick. It was always like this at the end of something. They were the biggies of the little school, but at the end of summer they would be littlest at the big school, and they would be split into clever and thick and nothing would be the same again. And every week now she kept getting taller and learning more, and being pushed further away from something and closer to something else, and there was nothing she could do about it.

Then she heard the shouts, felt the stir like a hot wind across the playground. A rammy, a fecht. A swarm of children spilled out between the bike sheds and the wall, and more were running to join them.

She sooked the last of the milk. Nothing to do with her. It was all stupid and cruel and if you got involved it caught you in its dirty excitement.

She heard the shout, then a squeal that could only be Porky, and she was running towards the sheds with the empty bottle in her hand.

Seona waved her over and they grabbed poles and balanced on the cycle racks and there was Porky in the middle. Someone had torn his white shirt and it hung away from his shoulder and stomach and you could see the white rolls of fat. He was greiting, kicking at anyone who lunged towards him but there were too many.

She craned her neck and saw Spotty Fraser catch one arm and Big Eck grab the other and the boys closed in. Beside her Seona was jigging with excitement.

'Isn't it awfy?' she said, but her eyes were shining. 'Should someone run and tell the teacher?'

'Caa the breeks aff him!' Maggie Graham shouted and then the girls were all shouting 'Breeks! Breeks!' And there was Fando cool as anything sitting on the wall off to the side, just watching with no expression on his face and scraping his nails with the flick knife and doing nothing one way or another. She knew why but already she was jumping down.

She grabbed Big Eck, who was smaller than her anyway, pulled and tripped him and he fell into the other boys.

'Leave him alane!' she was shouting and she swiped Spotty Fraser and he let go Porky's other arm and then the focus turns like a burning glass on her. Someone pushed, she stumbled and her hair was yanked. She whirls round to shake off hands tugging at her dress, glimpses Seona with her mouth open and Fando leaning forward on the wall and she sees the knife click up in his hand and then her head's banged and a sharp pain in her side. She's bounced off somebody and Porky flushed with success comes to thump her again. To hit her! And she'd saved him!

As she gapes at him he kicks her in the shin and the sickness runs to her throat and Fando is sliding smoothly down off the wall. Her right arm strikes up with the bottle still in her hand. Porky falls down and blood flows from his nose so red over the torn white shirt. Then Dewar shouts from the steps and everyone scatters and Porky is running bawling out the school gates and she will never see him again except in sweating dreams.

Fando pulled the bottle from her hand, lobbed it over the wall and slid the knife back in his pocket.

'Sure you're the wild one,' he said and looked at her in the way she'd imagined lately. Her brother, her equal. He was holding her arm and she felt the tears prickling.

'I'm not, I'm not,' she muttered and shook him off because it was all wrong, and she ran head down for the toilets before she was sick.

Summer days are here again, The birds are on the wing. God's goodness and His loving grace unconsciously they sing.

It was cool and dim in the little assembly hall. Through the high windows she saw the tops of the hot trees shimmering. She'd always loved this song with its stroking words and now it made her feel ill. Perhaps she was ill. Perhaps they'd let her go away and hide behind the waterfall till she got better.

Fando slid in behind her and she felt something long and smooth pushed into her hand. *The tall trees in the greenwood, the meadows where we play . . .*

'You keep this, colleen,' he whispered. 'We're off to Blair for the fruit-picking. 'Bye.'

She nodded and slipped it into her duffel bag as she felt him go.

Then it was time to go up on stage, curtsy and get her English prize from the lady in the blue hat and try not to drop *The Adventures of Huckleberry Finn*, slidey and book-smelling in her hand.

She sat under the hawthorn tree at the top of High Field. She could hear faint laughter and shouting and whistling at dogs from where the gypsies were leaving.

She wrapped her arms round her knees and laid her head on them. She'd left the wee school.

She reached into her duffel bag and pulled out Fando's

present. She stroked the white bone whistle, ran her fingers round the rough little holes, pushed her tongue into the whistling slot. She blew hard and got a high, thin shriek.

When he'd pushed it into her hand she'd been sure it was the knife. She'd wanted it to be the knife because it was wild and dangerous and something they'd shared, and then she could throw it back at him for being right about people, right about Porky and people and herself.

She waited for an hour under the tree where they hadn't kissed or fought or anything. She waited till she was very late for dinner and she'd learned to blow more softly and rap her fingers lightly along the holes and make something that wasn't quite music but her own, the sound of leaving things behind and a huge summer ahead.

She stopped playing. There were no more noises from by the river. She was hungry. She picked up her bag and ran home over the field, the whistle pumping up and down in her right hand, striking upwards with every second stride.

Porky Pig. Fando Fillamon. Seona. She feels them all.

Still lying on the couch, she remotes off the television and looks out the window. School will be out soon. She can feel the greasy jotter, she can still see the cock-eyed staples gleam.

But who the hell was Patrick Geddes?

She reaches for her notebook, a cigarette, and her tin whistle. And Stella shivers, feeling herself fall, like him, through a hole in someone else's memory.

She pulled on her dressing gown and pushed up the window. The stone sill was warm in the gloaming. In the distance a lawnmower was droning and the haze from the river was rising up towards the moon. Her father had gone out for company. She heard the click and scratch and then more violin music from downstairs as her mother put more records on. She'd play them for hours now. No wonder people thought they were all weird. Then she'd be weird. It sounded like weir, and water falling for ever.

She grasped the whistle between her teeth and with both hands free crawled out the window.

SPERMY McCLUNG

John Aberdein

McClung wisna a fisher name. Sae mebbe Spermy Jed McClung wisna a richt fisher? Ee fishit nivver on a Sunday, but ees boat wis steel. There wis nithin o'm tae luik at, yet ee coined siller like it fell fae the mune. A bandit.

McClung vrappit ees prop aff Foula ae nicht an wis ower the side like an otter, canife atween the teeth, likely. Big black boat, fite brakkin seas an the wee man McClung wis in aboot the thresh o rudder an net dishin oot surgery. Syne they shewed a fresh panel intil hir an were awa hame weil-fished afore daybreak, Jed wi a smashed chowk, the story ye'd heard. Sanct Bluidy Peter tae ees thieveless crew: an a coorse young spur-dug tae aabuddy else. Spur-dugs rippit yir nets: Spermy McClung snappit at yir starn, herdin aa the herrin ye suld hiv pursed intae ees ain lang rope an jaa.

Ee roamed an ee reenged. Nae clumpin seaboots for Spermy: Cuban heels. Ee tuik wife an kids tae Florida for a break, hid a blonde bit o stuff waitin'm in Sweden, an a snaa-fite Labrador trottin ahin'm in the Broch. A fine pine sauna waftit steam fae the boat's brig, an scattert aboot ees stateroom were *Men Only* an Melville, smudgy Polaroids o Erika, an a Kalashnikov assault rifle. Like ony Jack Flash that has come intil a coupla poun. Fit did ee cry ees boat? *Spare Me FR 69*.

* * *

Get that Buckiefuckin spratbasket ootfaeunder ma feet! Spermy yallochit fae the steel wing o the brig ae gousty Thursday mornin, as ee revved an rived ees wey hard throu the tethert fleet, burstin Dod Wiseman's breist-rope tae hash oot fish at the prompt man's price.

Wid splintert, ee duntit ees steel boo on the Ullapool pier, an a loon in a woolly hat gaed lowpin ashore tae lash.

McClung, that'll cost ye, wait yir turn! shoutit Wiseman. *This is nae a scramble, ye scumbag, there's a queue. Aabuddy's hivvin tae wait, some larries doon the road hiv got their snoots stuck in the snaa.*

Snaa, Wiseman, Ah dinna bide for ysh nor snaa. Gie yir auld traaler a rest, Ah'm in a hurry for a larry. Ah'm fleein tae Brussels the morn for meetins, an the crew's needin hame for a ride, that nae richt, boys? An ees mate on the deck, brave Baxter, lowered ees foreairm at the Buckier an strained it up judderin like a laundin jib. Nae aince but twice. Sae that wis it decidit. Fuckin rustler.

Oot in Brussels the Commissioners wir aa set tae sell the Scots fishers doon the Swanee. They sat roon in an oval wi the SFA reps, sip-sippan fae tumblers o table wattir. Drifter, ringer, traaler, purse, Mr McClung poundit oot figures, the laundins, the spin-aff, fit wis at stake. Oh they were genteel: back, forrard they leaned, they harkened.

The Chairman even said, strikin a note, *I myself would give an arm to help you, but there is fish not enough, you see, for everybody. It is our common resource, the fish, but we recognize becoming uncommon too? Yes?* An ee clinchit discouragement wi a smile, the lang peelikin, an pushed back ees mahogany chair.

Sae back cam McClung tae the Broch, ees twa kids cam rinnin doon the lang drive afore ee culd close the ranch-pole gate, an ee upendit them in ees twa airms tae ruggle their hair doon at a bowfin bouncin dug sae that Jason skirlt an Shareen grat. June cam scrunch in jeans an perm, an gave'm a saft kiss. *Hiya doll, the presents are in ower the back seat,* said Jed.

Eftir they cam oot the bedroom, an the kids still playin wi Action Man on the lang blue rug, they aa hid a splash in their pool, fit a caper. Rebel, the snaa-fite Lab, rolled wi the kids like a happy bear. The parents swam side-stroke facin each ither a filie, an Jed said, *We canna wait or the morn. Ah've tellt Baxter midnicht the nicht.* They ate their dennir in silence, Surf 'n' Turf, a feel name thon, the only scallop that ivver cam in throu surf wis Botticelli's.

Throu the Canal the *Spare Me* steamed, an roun bi the Sma Isles, landit five hunner cran sma herrin at Mallaig's jetty, syne oot tae save dues, rockan tae hir anker aff Rhum the Sabbath throu. A bonny day, spring, wi lang fite banners fleein fae the summit o Roneval.

Eftir brunch, Jed kittlit ees Kalashnikov on the brig railins an drew doon a black spot on a stag bi the shore. The hale day went quate. *Crack!* The reid stag huppt ees horns an sprang oot a twenty pace afore bucklin, hert-shot. It michtna be the season but Jed rolled on ees weet-suit an flippert in for'm, trailin a polyprop rope.

They cauchtna a herrin for twa weeks. The soonder wis blank, the sonar gave nivver a ping, they wir buggerit if they culd see a single solan closin its wings wi plungin beak.

Back tae the Broch cam McClung, the murmurin seen startit, ahint ees back as ee prowlt the pier, Rebel pad-paddin at ees heels. *Selfish divvel. Jist a killer. Nivver near the kirk. Swankin at hame in that bluidy ranch, the lazy c, an crew left tae starve for wiks. Ah'd like tae see'm beg on ees hunkers.*

Haurdlie the man ees fadder wis. Thon June's a prood bitch,
Ah'm sorry for the kids. Then a neebor clyped on ees dug.

Rebel hid worried her dochters she said, the wee lambs
ran tae the hoose an ane o their ganseys wis torn. Prima-
facie evidence for ony Sheriff an Rebel wis orderit tae be
putten doon inside a wik. Hertbroke wis Jed: sae aabuddy
thocht, as the days wore on, ee'd say *Fie* tae the Coort an
fecht the thing oot. Ee did warse bi far, as sune aabuddy
kent.

The postie wis comin tae the neebor, Mrs Guthrie's
villa, fan ee caucht sicht o a sickener on hir gate-post.
A muckle daud, a furrish lump: the fite dug's heid, aa
crimsie-collart! The wird flew roon but nivver a buddy
ootspowk.

Sae Spermy left for Sweden wi a skeleton crew, got a
grander power-block fittit, dilly-dallied wi the camera an
Erika till they wir baith scunnert, and went hame tae pick
up the boys. Twa days later they shot fifty miles aist o the
Bressa licht, a great circle o net trailin doon a hunder
faddom. Fan ye pickit up yir end an the boddom wis
pursed nae fish culd mak scape, an nither they did, nae
herrin this time, nae even machrel, but flamin sprats.

Fuckin sprats! screamed Baxter. *They'll mash on us!*

It'll tak us a day, said Jed. *We'll hae tae shak aa bi haun.*

The truth wis that herrin aye swam in a purse weil-
content till ye got them alangside an sookit them up. But
sprats were that wee they dashed their snooties throu the
sma mesh tae get snared bi the gills, an either bided like
Stoics or droont quick in shock.

The net cam aboord bi the pouer o the Triplex, a rub-
ber-clad affair wi three drums, a hydraulic mungle. Let a
dizzen o deid sprats throu the rollers tho, an aa their yly
juices wid squidge an the net stert tae skite. Sae ivvery last
sprat hid tae be plapped back in the owshin bi the crew

raxin for net, an gruppin an shakkin. As coorse as rake cockles on a frozent strand wi yir fingers ootstreiked like a harra. An it wis either shakshak, inch the net in – for twenty-fower oors – or slash clean awa an ging hame tae the jeers.

They haalt, an better haalt, an shook an weary shook, an the wee man McClung stude on the wing o the brig, warkin the gleamin Triplex, draain the silvert net slaw fae the wattir like remuvin a barbit arra. The day wis a lang day, simmer, an the gulls squallochit an fed an squalled mair angry fan they culdna lift aff, sae swam bloatit.

Nicht passit quick in the spratshimmer, thoosans o scaly-kins faain plooterin back in the skinklan sea like the gut-heaves o a drunken warld. An wi gulls full up, an the sea gone quate, a guff cam aff the phosphort glut, sic a reek up yir nebstrous, till ye near puked yirsel. Fan day cam back roon, Jed sent the crew ben the cabin for het mugs o broth, meat wid barely bide doon fan ye warkit like thon, yir airms aboot crucified, yir belly athwart jist ached wi the strain.

Jed bade on brig-watch, sweyin, liftin the hunkie ower ees neb tae sup fae a bottlie wattir. Ee jaloused jist afore the lads left'm that a lirk hid twistit at the vera moo o the purse-block. 'Twid seerly be better tae lat hir drap back an strachten, afore a ticht fistick fouled up the warks. Oot on the wing ee went, ettlin wi ees free haun tae yark the lirk free. It cam awa fine an ee pit the reid knob aheid, upgroanin the net fae the spratswallen wattir.

But na, the net wis still for plyan hir tricks, sae ee streicht up an tuggit. O but man's fingers are nae mair than sprats fan aa's deen; Jed's haun wis sune snarled in a snorl o nylon. Rax back ee culdna, on the tips o ees Cubans, wi an airm strachtened up like some pee-ma-breeks scholar.

Baxter, helpies, Baxter! The gulls thrasht alang on the flesch-fillt wattir, *Baxter!*

Intae the rollers fan ees haun slippit sae numb, ee wis feart, ee mustna ging numb, it wid be the easiest thing. Fannyaboot screamin an ye'd sune black-oot, loll saft in a dwaam, till they gazed on yir napper like a chappit neep.

McClung upswung ees Cuban boots hard on the stanchion. Braced back. Man's wiriness against the rollers' endless virr, ee yarkit doon, felt ees shoulder ging thlop. Syne ee groond roon sair on the toom socket, nithin but skin an . . . ivver rived a live scallop apairt? Ivver hid cause tae rive yir ainsel? Up wi yir boots tae the bracket, tuck yir neb ticht tae yir troosers, an roar doon oot an awa!

Cauld kind the deck. O, ee hid rippit ees airm aff. In its ain sleeve, nae even lanely, headin aff heavenward. 'Twid nivver dae. Jed stude, admonished the rollers, an pit ees life on rewind. As if in obleegement ees left airm cam back, unstrung itsel fae the purse-strings, drappin saft tae the deck. McClung bent. *Ah'm doon tae ma last oxter. An that's far Ah'll pit it. Like a brakken French loaf,* ee thocht.

Fan Spermy kicked open the door o the cabin, the boys stared – *Gad's sake!* The gruel froze in their moo. Christ, the crimsie wis spirtin throu the clasp o ees fingers!

Ee flang ees auld airm doon on the bunk. *Weil, boys, that's ma big days in fishin ower.*

Unsneckin the first-aid box, the mate matit morphine an needle but ees thoom stertit trummlin atap o the plunger. *Fa-far'll Ah pit it, Jed, far'll ah pi . . . ?*

Pit it far it fits, min, dae ye think Ah'll fuckin feel it?

Eftir, in the chopper divertit tae Aiberdeen wi McClung's mortified airm lyan in a fish-box o meltin ysh, the leal Baxter tried tae comfort ees skipper.

Did ye really hack thon dug's heid aff? said Baxter.

Na, ah tuik'm for a dander, gave'm a digestive, syne pit the barrel tae ees lug file ee wis happy an chowin. Corpse an gun Ah'd nae furder eese for, intae the Ugie wi them, syne plunk wi Reb's heid on the wifie's palin. Gin ye wint a deid dug, this is fit a deid dug luiks like, wis ma wird. Eh? Ye jist canna lat onybuddy kill yir ain dug!

Stitcht an transfused, Spermy sune cam hame, lat ees shouder slope vacant, made luve on ees guid side but *fell ahin wi the foreplay* as ee aye eesed tae say. Dod Wiseman phoned, nice o'm, an ee got a card fae Brussels. Ee swam in ees pool an syne snorkellt the skerries, tae salve ees wound an jist keep at the fish. *Ye can aye ram somethin up yir auld string vest,* said Jed, an lauchit. *Tho Ah'll nivver tak a labster missan a claa. We one-airmed bandits maun stick thegither.*

Nae lang eftir ee wis awa up Shetland, ae haun on the spokit wheel an the ghaist o the ither dirlin. The fleet were aa roon, purlin ower the deep marks, waitin the herrin tae rise. The boats kept their distance, haivin up an doon on the sunset swall. Dark fell an Jed's fishin licht went up.

Chuck awa! shoutit Spermy McClung, an lat it aa dance oot, tae the eternal funeral o fresh fish an siller.

THE CURAM

Lorn Macintyre

A blind man could have found his way to MacCallum's, the baker's shop on Main Street, behind the memorial clock. The people in the flats above left their windows open overnight so that the fragrances from the first batch of bread wakened them.

MacCallum wore a white cap without a brim as he wielded the long wooden shovel at the oven, lifting out the risen loaves. His arms were bare, the tattooed anchors showing that he had been at sea as a young man. In the summer there were queues from the yachts in the bay for his bread when he fired his ovens an hour earlier. MacCallum was one of the last native Gaelic speakers left in the town, and old people went in for the pleasure of his conversation as well as his pastries.

On Saturday night MacCallum got very drunk in the pub with the steamship engraved on the window. Sometimes he got embroiled in fights, and these fists that had pummelled the dough into little rolls pulverized a face he didn't take to. But on Monday morning he was down at the shop, getting the ovens going, and didn't touch a drop till the next weekend.

My sister and I were coming home late with heavy baskets and stained mouths from picking blackcurrants on the path to the lighthouse. We balanced our burdens on the stone seats round the memorial clock before going home along Main Street.

'MacCallum's shop's on fire!' my sister shouted.

We ran across the street and saw the flames coming from the open oven, running down the pole to the floor where MacCallum was lying. The fire brigade broke in his window and carried him out into the night air. He had stayed late to make a wedding cake of rich fruit for a local. It wasn't the smoke that had killed him, but a heart attack.

His widow put the shop up for sale, and everyone had to eat tasteless wrapped bread from the mainland, and cakes with icing like china glaze that came on the ferry. Then my mother heard in the Cooperative that the bakery had been taken by an English couple.

They came in a tall van with their furniture to a house up the hill. The bakery was renovated. The old ovens that dated from the time before there were any cars on the island were ripped out and new ones fed by gas installed. Because of screens you couldn't see the new baker at work through the window.

I went in on the first day of business with Mother. There was a lit counter containing all kinds of confections. The bread was in racks above, in strange shapes, dough that had been knotted into figures of eight, elongated into French sticks, slapped into circular crusties dusted with flour.

The new baker was as good as MacCallum, maybe even better because he had a bigger variety. It was said that he had been trained as a pastry chef in a big London hotel before opening his own shop. The Quintons were quiet people. They were both in the shop even earlier than MacCallum. While Mrs Quinton washed out the lit counter her husband fired the pristine ovens and slid in the trays of pale dough. But the aromas didn't rise to the open windows above to waken the people. Instead they were ducted away to the back of the shop.

There wasn't any Gaelic spoken in the shop now, and no more fights in the pub because Quinton wasn't a drinker. It was hard to say what he was. He didn't go to any of the three churches in the town, yet he and his wife were never seen on a Sunday. They kept to themselves, and the curtains of their house at the top of the town stayed shut.

They sold their produce at reasonable prices, and in the evening the lit counter was empty, the racks of loaves cleared. The ovens were scrubbed out, the tiles mopped. The Quintons put up bills for dances and whist drives in their window, but they never went to any functions, not even the dance held on the pier on regatta night, when there would be a hundred yachts in the bay.

One morning I was in the shop with the basket for our bread order. The boy in front of me was handed a loaf half out of its bag and he swore as he took it.

'What did you say?' Mrs Quinton asked, still holding the other end of the French stick.

'It was hot,' the boy complained.

'You'll go to a place hotter than that oven through there if you use words like that,' Mrs Quinton warned him before she relinquished the loaf.

'I hope you didn't hear the word he used,' Mrs Quinton said as she served me.

I had heard the word plenty of times, when my friends gathered round the memorial clock in the early evening to try to attract boys, using the sample lipsticks that came taped to the magazines they bought, with advice on their skin and their hearts.

'Are you a believer?' Mrs Quinton asked me.

I was so taken aback that I almost dropped the crusty loaf.

'I don't know what you mean.'

'Do you believe in Jesus Christ?' Mrs Quinton enquired.

I hadn't given the matter much thought. My parents had made us go to Sunday school, but the church up the brae was always chilly, and my eyes always wandered to the bright day beyond the stained-glass windows. At the age of twelve we had rebelled, and there was no more attendance.

My father talked a lot about the history of the town. There had been five churches at one time, serving a population of four hundred. He could remember the procession along Main Street on a Sunday morning to the big church with the tower, but the lead had fallen from its windows, and there were crossed planks and a Danger sign at the front door. The Baptist church further along was only open once a month for half a dozen old people who had to be helped out of cars, and one of them was on a zimmer. Attendance was declining drastically in the other churches.

'I don't go to church,' I told Mrs Quinton.

I expected to have the crusty loaf snatched back, but she leaned over the lit counter of confections and dropped the bread into my basket.

'I'm not talking about church-going,' she said. 'You don't have to go to a church to meet Jesus Christ. He's everywhere, even in this shop.'

As she said this she flung her arm dramatically, as if she was dispatching an inferior loaf back to its baker. The screen was open and Mr Quinton was standing in front of the open oven, with its line of little blue jets. He was wearing a tall white hat, and held up the bread pole as if it were a bishop's staff.

'Jesus Christ is everywhere!' he called through to me in a singsong voice.

I was troubled as I left the shop. My life seemed suddenly to go flat, and I walked home in the shadows of the buildings while my sister and her friends sat in the sun round the memorial clock with young men in blue boots off a yacht that had just come into the bay.

'Mr and Mrs Quinton say that Jesus Christ is everywhere,' I suddenly blurted out over supper.

We were having mackerel, and Father looked as if he were choking on a bone.

'Say that again.'

I said it again, slowly, feeling a strange shiver in my spine.

'I haven't heard that for a long time, not since I was a boy,' Father said. 'What a pity none of you has Gaelic.'

'I'm sorry you had to marry a monolingual wife, Archie,' Mother said wearily.

'I'm not blaming you,' he said, covering her hand. 'There's a word in Gaelic, *curam*. It means trust or command. But it's got another meaning.'

He told us the story over the scattered bones of the mackerel, and the potato skins I should have eaten to build iron into my body, as Mother said.

It was the time when the steamers came into the pier, crowded with tourists. They had an hour ashore, and they left a lot of money behind.

'It didn't go into the plates of the churches, that's for certain,' Father said.

'Where did it go?' my sister asked.

'Into cars and three-piece suites. That was also the beginning of the decline of Gaelic.'

'Don't get on to that subject again, Archie,' Mother warned him. 'It isn't good for your blood pressure.'

One day, Father said, a man had come down the steamer gangway with a black suit buttoned up to his Adam's apple, and a portmanteau bag. He didn't go back on board when the whistle sounded. He was a preacher from an island further north, and his Gaelic was harsh and abrasive.

'But once he got into a pulpit, that didn't matter,'

Father recalled. 'He had brought the *curam*, you see. The town's drinkers and some of the most disreputable women were falling on their knees on Main Street, saying that they had heard the call of Jesus Christ. The man in the next croft to my father was scything one day when the *curam* got him, like a wasp sting. He fell on the scythe blade and almost severed an artery. You couldn't get a seat in the biggest church.'

'I don't see what this has to do with the Quintons,' I said.

'The Quintons have brought the *curam* with them,' Father explained. 'They've kept quiet up until now, but they're trying to push their born-again Christianity. I'm not even sure that it's safe to eat their cakes,' he added, staring at the tempting plate with a straight face. He leaned across and touched my nose with his finger. 'Take care you don't get the *curam*, young lady, because you can't get rid of it like lipstick.'

I began to look forward to going into the bakery, and hung about at the plate-glass window till the shop was clear. Mrs Quinton gave me another chapter, waving her hands behind the counter.

'Oh you look the type that will be visited by Jesus Christ,' she told me. 'He will come anytime, even in the night.'

'Praise be,' her husband said, striking the staff of his oven shovel on the tiles.

'How will I know?' I asked as I took the warm crusty loaf with its many grooves.

'Oh, you'll know,' she assured me. 'It'll come like lightning, and you'll be filled with a radiance.'

'Like this,' Mr Quinton sang from the back, turning up the blue jets in the oven into hissing flames.

'Come up to the house one night,' Mrs Quinton whispered across the lit counter.

I can still feel the crunch of the gravel under my shoes

as I went up the drive to the secluded house with its closed curtains. Mr Quinton answered the door. He was wearing a Fair Isle pullover, and I followed him into the big sitting room where Mrs Quinton was waiting with a plate of their own cakes.

I started to go up to the Quintons every night while my sister looked for romance at the memorial clock. I couldn't sleep when I came back. My bedroom seemed to be filled with a radiance that wasn't from the lamps on Main Street. One very hot night I went downstairs to the bookcase.

'What are you doing?' my sister asked, coming into the sitting room in her trendy pyjamas to sprawl in a chair.

'Reading the Bible,' I told her.

'What's getting into you?' she challenged me. 'There are some very nice boys staying in the youth hostel.'

'I'm not interested,' I said. 'I've had the call.'

'Who called you?' she asked eagerly, sitting up in the chair. 'Is it someone I know?'

'I doubt that,' I said, and resumed reading Revelations.

Next night when I came back down the hill my parents were waiting for me in the sitting room.

'Where have you been?' Mother confronted me.

'Up at the Quintons.'

'And is this where you go every night?' Father asked.

I nodded.

'What do you go up there for?' Mother said in alarm.

'Be calm, Flora,' Father warned her. 'We need to get at the truth. 'Marsali, why do you go to the Quintons?'

'Because they asked me up,' I answered.

'And what do you do when you're up there?' he asked patiently.

'We hold hands.'

'You hold hands?' He sounded alarmed. 'With who?'

'With Mr and Mrs Quinton. There's nobody else there,' I told him.

'And what do you do when you hold hands?' he asked.

'We sing and dance.'

He was looking at Mother.

'Give us an example,' he requested.

'I can't,' I said bashfully. 'We go round and round and sing about being saved by Jesus Christ. Mrs Quinton has a tambourine.'

'And what else?' he asked.

'We watch videos.'

His eyes narrowed.

'What kind of videos?'

'Videos from America,' I said.

'Oh – Archie,' Mother moaned.

'Hush, Flora,' he told her. 'What kind of videos? And when you answer, don't turn your face away.'

'Videos of evangelists,' I explained. 'They preach to huge audiences in the Hollywood Bowl. Benny Epps converts hundreds of sinners.'

'And does Mr Quinton do anything else?' he asked.

'What do you mean?'

'Does he touch you?' Father asked, watching Mother again.

'He holds my hand and hugs me.'

'He hugs you,' Father said, his voice changing. 'Does he kiss you?'

'No,' I protested.

'Does he touch you anywhere?'

I had read about that kind of thing in one of my sister's magazines.

'If you mean does he touch me in private places, he does not,' I said, looking him straight in the eye. 'Mr Quinton is not that kind of person.'

'This is big-scale *curam*,' Father said to Mother. 'It's even

68

got into the bread.' He turned to me. 'You are never to go near the Quintons' house again. Is that understood?'

'Are you going to deprive me of the comfort of Jesus Christ?' I asked him. It didn't sound like my own voice coming from my own mouth.

'Your sister will do the shopping,' Mother said.

'She is the one who betrayed me,' I said bitterly. 'How many pieces of silver did you give her for lipstick?'

'That's no way to speak to your mother,' Father said angrily. 'She loves you and cares about you. Now I'm going to book us all a holiday in Spain. I'll get last-minute bargains.'

For the rest of that week I had bad dreams in which someone was beating me over the head with a tambourine and shouting that I would go to hell. I waited outside the shop until the Quintons locked up.

'I can't come up any more,' I informed them.

'Why not?' Mrs Quinton asked.

'I'm going on holiday abroad.'

'And will we see you when we come back?' Mrs Quinton asked.

'No,' I told them, looking at my shoes. 'My parents forbid it.'

'Because we are spreading the word of Jesus Christ,' Mrs Quinton said sadly.

'He could walk on water, but he has never been to this island,' Mr Quinton said.

'Where did you first meet Jesus Christ?' I asked.

'We had a very successful bakery in the south. We used to stay open late, and our teenage daughter cycled home. One night she went under a lorry.' Mrs Quinton's voice had dropped to a whisper. 'I was on tranquillizers, but I couldn't cope. Why our innocent child? I kept asking. What sense was there in God taking her from us in that terrible way? Daniel was drinking heavily and our bakery was shut.'

'A bottle of vodka a day,' Mr Quinton said sadly.

'Our regular customers went elsewhere, and we were almost bankrupt. On the day I was due to go into a mental institution, when I was lying crying my heart out on a sofa, I suddenly felt the spirit of Jesus Christ filling the room, like the fragrance of newly risen bread,' Mrs Quinton explained. 'I called Daniel through and he sensed it too, didn't you, Daniel?'

Mr Quinton nodded.

'Daniel stopped drinking and I didn't need any more treatment. We came up here to make a new life for ourselves, and to spread the word about being reborn through Jesus Christ,' Mrs Quinton continued.

'And when we met you, it seemed like a gift from him, you were so like her,' Mr Quinton added. His eyes were brimming with tears. 'But we can't stay here now.'

The Quintons' furniture went away in a tall van. My sister wore a very skimpy bikini on the beach in Spain, and I took a sick turn. The baker's is now a gift shop, and they keep tartan souvenir dolls in the cold ovens. There are pebbles from Iona in the lit counter. The bread comes from the mainland, a day old, white and dry in paper. And I am getting Gaelic lessons from Father.

MANITOBA

Lizbeth Gowans

She could hear her father's raised voice as she passed the window and a moment later on the doorstep she was shoved out of his way as he stormed from the house, tacketty boots thundering along the brick path. Coming or going, the sound of those boots on the path was a daily pointer to the sort of mood he was in. On a fine April day, if the lambing was going well, and his stomach wasn't bothering him, the footsteps might be easy, sauntering home or leaving for a walk with the dogs. There might be a pause as he stopped to gaze at the Pentlands. Listeners inside would be grateful for a sense of wellbeing. But on a bad day, the boots came fast and someone soon was about to pay dearly. Then, as today, the row would take place, abuse would be flung, and the thunder-boots departed, leaving behind the usual quaking.

Inside, she found her mother wiping her eyes with the end of one of her apron bands, the cleanest part, she once said, when Ella asked why they always had their bairn tears wiped with it. Her mother turned on Ella her grave, maternal what-will-become-of-you look. 'I doot we'll no be here long.'

'Oh? Why's that?' As if she didn't know fine well.

'Your faither's got it inty his heid that he's no appreciatit by them at the Big Hoose.'

'It doesn't take much to put that into his head with

71

anyone. Why's he like that always? Look at him the other night.'

In the absence of her father, Ella felt free to expand her exasperation. 'Asking *us* to tell him how much *we* appreciated him – like ... like some flaming old King Lear.'

Her mother began to pull laundry down from the pulley and fold it. 'Aye, well, you certainly put his gas in a peep telling him you appreciated him just as much as a daughter should.'

Her mother's tone was wry enough to leave her wondering whether she was being commended or gently chastised.

'Well, I mean, really, Mum. Why does he ask such things? And, anyway, if it's the Big House he's not pleased with, why's he shouting at you?'

'Because, I suppose, he canny go shoutin' at them.'

'That's not fair.'

'No. But it's his nature. Just human nature, Ella.'

'Human nature? Ha!' She shouted aloud a contempt she'd been nursing all her life. 'Well, if that's human nature, I'll tell you something. I hate it. I'll *always* ... absolutely ... anathematize it!'

Her mother laughed at her. 'Anathema*tize*, eh? You mean, curse it?'

'Aye. Just that.'

Her mother laughed again, suddenly light-hearted. 'Here. Give's a hand wi' this sheet.'

They took single corners and folded, stepped together, matched double corners, folded, matched, smoothed, till the sheet could be handled easily with a last folding over her mother's forearm. Then they went quietly about their other orderly ways at that time of day with a meal to prepare for a family, no matter what. Soon, drawn by the peaceful, familiar noises below, the boys and wee Jean crept back downstairs for their tea. And soon, too, the dreaded boots could be heard returning, but now they were slack and weary-sounding, like their wearer when he came in and took his place at the silent table.

Ella didn't dare ask what form this lack of Big House appreciation had taken to offend their father so, but she wondered if it had anything to do with Jessie Menzies' boast at school that day that *her* father had got a 'harvest bonus' from the Boss. There had been no such talk in their house, at any rate. That would do it, of course, for Andra Yuill had been born on the lookout for the subtlest signs of preference, so no wonder something as public as this had thrown him into such a passion.

She stole a glance at his face and saw how worn out he was with it, and something else, something cowed, and she felt both angry and sorry, angry that she was sorry, for why did he always have to regard another man's good fortune as some kind of slight to him?

All the same, she understood. She only had to think of Peg Wishart getting the art prize this year to understand, and Peg was a good pal. How much worse if it were some-one you despised, as her father did yon Menzies. Human nature again, naturally. It seemed to her more and more the seat of all that was ignoble, a tyrannical force to be fought at all costs.

Briefly, the way she often had a counter-thought to most of her strongest thoughts, she wondered what could be put in place of the tyrant. That gave her a queer vision of her father shoved out of his home, his boots rattling helplessly on the brick path, and then of her mother coming after him with soft strokings, smoothing his clothes, matching his wildly flung-out arms with her own, but gently, palms to palm, folding his hands to her breast. Ella stared at her plate, so close was she to the vision and to tears. But it was wee Jean who broke the strain of the silent table by starting to cry, blaming her favourite pie for the way she felt. 'I dinny *like* this yin. I dinny *like* it,' she cried, until Ella took it away and her mother gathered the child in her arms.

It had happened before – before they moved to this place, before they moved to the place before that, and before that again. Ella had hoped that here, back in the Pentlands where her father had been born and where he had courted their mother, they might come to rest, at least for more than a year.

Peg Wishart asked Ella one day why she had lived in so many different places. There seemed a truly genuine interest in her question, instead of the usual sneery suggestion of shiftiness, or failure, that even teachers evinced.

'Well,' Ella replied, 'if you think about it, my father is part of an ancient tradition going back to the Bible.'

'Oh? What tradition do you mean, Ella?'

'The – eh – nomadic tradition. Shepherds were like that then. They still are, in Scotland, some of them, like my father.'

Peg was quietly impressed by this, although she did point out that it wouldn't suit *her* to be always having to leave known friends and teachers and get used to new ones.

'Oh aye. There's that. But, Peg, you know, we get to travel and see far-flung bits of the country – which is good for our geography.'

As she uttered this, Ella wondered if Peg would next ask in what manner they did all this travelling. Would she tell her about the sheep-float, with the three-piece suite packed in last for herself and the bairns to sit in with only the slats to look through at the countryside? Would she tell her how Davy and Wattie, at a stop in Crieff once, stuck their faces against a slat and bleated like wee lambs to the horror of several passers-by who noticed? She decided she'd leave Peg with the dignified biblical picture of their family's wanderings, in the hope that such a view might get passed around and even that some would say *that* explained why Ella Yuill was so good at geography and knew the names of every shire in the British Isles, not to mention every state in North America – Ella Yuill, the learned nomad.

For a while after the Big House slight, nothing more was said on the subject but at the end of each day's work her father seemed more depressed, her mother more anxious, than any time before. Then one evening, she overheard her mother say as she was about to go and milk, 'Andra. Come tae the byre wi' me a minute.'

The byre was a fine inner sanctum, being quiet, warm, lamplit, smelling of cream and hay. Talk there tended to be thoughtful. Ella waited for a sign, some word of betterment, of hope. Sure enough, the word came, fairly bursting from Davy's mouth as he ran to meet her after school one cold November day.

'Manitoba!' he shouted. 'Manitoba, Ella! We're gaun tae Ma-ni-to-ba!'

Enchanted with the syllables of the name, it became in his play at home his new battle cry as he leaped over the doorstep on his way out to charge at the life of another day.

They were all warned not to breathe a word to anyone yet. All was not arranged, letters had to be written, replies waited for, but from that day the household grew cheerful. When light in heart, Andra Yuill liked to sing, and now in the evening he took wee Jean on his knee and gave them 'Springtime in the Rockies'. Then her mother rendered 'Hame o' Mine', the famous exile song that irritated Ella because it was so often sung at gatherings of folk who'd never been exiled in their lives and yet it wrung tears from

75

all listeners, including herself, right from the very first line, 'I sit and I gaze o'er the wild lonely prairie.'

You heard stories all the time since the war of folk emigrating, with help from the government, for a brand-new destiny. Their uncle and aunt and cousins from Edinburgh had spent a whole month on a ship taking them to Australia along with a load of other Scottish families.

At first, defending herself against the hopeful sentiment that these stories, and now her own family's dreams, engendered in human nature, Ella stayed cool about Manitoba until it occurred to Davy one day to wonder where exactly this place was. She got out her school atlas to show him and, long after he'd run off to play, remarking only that it was awful pink and that a place called Manitoba should be 'a kinna drum colour', she remained gazing at the atlas.

Springtime there would be very far from the Rockies indeed, but the wild lonely prairie would surely bloom with field flowers as far as the eye could see. And look how the eastern boundary line began in the south to parallel the western one and then veered away to the Hudson Bay, opening up the province to the shore line, with M-A-N-I-T-O-B-A printed across the mouth.

What did it mean, the name? She looked in the dictionary and murmured the definitions aloud.

'Manitoba: from the Cree, *manitoopeek*, "divine water". That'll be referring to that huge lake, Lake Winnipeg. Here's another word. *Manito*: in the Algonquin thought to mean "to surpass"; also, a natural force, of good or evil, regarded with religious awe. Hm. Fancy that.'

Whereas Davy's wild chantings of the name and her parents' musical fantasies of a far country had left her cold, these factual Indian-based words and meanings filled her with excitement. She alone had discovered the true Manitoba and what a real Manitoban was.

From that moment, her imagination was alive with tall Indian-looking folk moving through long, wind-blown prairie grasses and flowers, fishing, bathing and being blessed by their divine water, in a life of surpassing beauty. Their flocks and herds had vast spaces to graze in, and their families (outside the city of Winnipeg, at least) wandered freely the length and breadth of the province from the Hudson Bay to North Dakota and the borders of Saskatchewan. It seemed to her quite possible that, after a time of transplantation, human nature itself might become pure Manitoban, fit to be blessed, not cursed.

As winter came on, a time when the field flocks had to be fed daily with laboriously sliced turnips and bales of hay, when livestock under cover required much tending and cleaning out, and life on the farm was at its least cheerful, her father remained in good spirits, working with purpose, and the boots on the brick path sounded an easy daily tread. Her mother wrote more letters – arrangements still on the go, evidently – and she sang around the house. There had never been such a long period of peacefulness in their lives, it seemed. Ella nodded to herself, knowing fine what was behind it, grateful for it. They didn't even have to talk about it. It was just there, like ... like ... that *manito*, the natural spirit, of good in this case. It would see them right through the dreary days of winter into the spring when, at the May Term, they would set sail from the Port of Leith. Then it would be *farewell tae the Pentlands, farewell tae the Forth, farewell tae Auld Reekie, braw land o' my birth.*

It was during a February evening visit from one of the elders of the kirk, Mr Parker, come to leave communion cards, that Davy and Wattie let the name slip, and everything broke.

'A wee bird,' said Mr Parker, the first to get wind of any

change in the district air, 'tells me you'll be leaving us in May for another clime.'

Alarmed, Ella was surprised at how calmly her mother and father took this. 'Aye,' her father said. 'I'm away tae a better bit.'

Davy and Wattie nudged each other and sang slyly together, 'Ma-ni-to-ba, here I come.' And ran out of the room when everyone looked at them.

'You're never going there!' Mr Parker said.

Her parents gave wee smiles at each other. Ella waited to hear their brave announcement, relieved that now it could be known by all.

'Aye, well,' her father was saying, 'we thocht aboot it for a while. An' I'll say this much. It did us guid tae entertain it, ye ken. But no, it's Ayrshire for us. A ferm on its ain, lookin' ower the Firth o' Clyde. I'll be my ain boss there. A braw place . . .'

He was still describing the beauties of Ayrshire as Ella left the room, shouting to herself that it wasn't true, he was just spinning a story to put Mr Parker off. Later, when she finally asked her mother, and found it was all too true, she could hardly speak for chagrin.

'But why didn't . . . ? How could you let me . . . ?'

'What's wrong wi' ye, Ella?'

'I wanted . . . I thought . . . You should've *told* me.'

'We only found oot this mornin' for certain.'

'What? That we weren't going to Manitoba?'

'No, no. Aboot the Ayrshire place.'

'And what,' Ella said accusingly, 'about Manitoba?'

Her mother looked a little vague as she bent over to tidy a cushion crushed by Mr Parker. 'Oh yes, well, like your father said, it was a fine thing to think aboot when we were sae low. It served its purpose. Folk need a lift at times, Ella, tae help them tae . . . It's just hu—'

'Don't *tell* me that!' Ella cried and ran for the front

door in her stocking soles. Desperate to get out, she stuck her feet into the nearest footwear, a pair of her father's tacketty boots. She stumbled noisily along the brick path to the byre where she kicked them off and climbed into the low rafters to sit with the cows, overwhelmingly stuck with her human nature and, much worse than any exile, sorely missing Manitoba.

CHASING STALLIONS

Kathryn Heyman

Thelma Berry was ninety centimetres wide. Exactly. I knew, because I measured the doorway where she got stuck and had to turn sneaky sideways and crab herself into the front lounge. No, not the front lounge, just the lounge. Only one room in this new place – not even a house, just a flat, and tiny. One room for eating and watching telly and farting all over my stupid sister, who just sits there anyway and lets you do it, she is so boring stupid boring. One toilet and two bedrooms. One for my mum and my sister (Kari the spastic) and one for me. I laughed till I spewed up the day Thelma got stuck in the door. Thelma was one of Mum's new fatlady friends. All walloping great laughs they were together.

Mum was suddenly new and loud without Dad, not cramped and breathless like before. Fat frigging libbers, Dad said. Mum laughed like a fatlady now: hahahHaHa-HAHAHAAAAWOo oh dear. All around the red laminex table, drinking beer sometimes. Ladies never drank beer. All yelling and laughing like the wind was pulling it out of them. Thought they'd fly off to the sky sometimes, the way they rocked back with their mouths open and cacking. Men, they'd say, and: *Rather have a cucumber*. Cack cack cack hahahAHAHAWo dear. My sister says she likes to hear Mum laugh, but it makes me shiver. Girls are weak chuck 'em in the creek. I am homesick for Dad and Mum says no, no going back only forwards.

Before, back in Boolaroo, we had: four bedrooms, two bathrooms (if you count the outside toilet), two lounge (one front, one back), one dining, one garden, one laundry. Two cocker spaniels, four mongrel pups, three cats, one snake (Diamond), three horses and one bird (a cocky). And once I killed a mouse. Oh, and once there were a couple of starlings in the roof which Dad strangled. He had feathers and blood on his hands and his face was bright and gleamy. He spoke loud loud loud after, all day. They're pests, they're no good to anyone, starlings. Bloody nuisances. Like that time Fosters the cat had kittens and Dad wrung their necks and burned them. All bright and shiny-eyed again he was, and hard. The next day I took them out of the fire, little black bodies with twisted crooked necks. I played dodgems with the corpses, but they had no wheels and left marks on my hands, so I chucked them and went into the station instead.

Sam (who I call Sam and not Constable Wright because my dad is the Senior Detective Sergeant and we own the police station) said Dad was out the back. I couldn't find him, like I sometimes can't – he just goes places, my dad. Inside was Mum. Cooking for the prisoners. We had a prison in the backyard. White. A white prison. With a big thick door and some little scrinchy bars at the top. Dad says it's just a lock-up. For drunks and ratbags and nooligans, which I have to be careful not to turn into one of them. So, Mum cooks for them. No, she did used to cook for them, then in Boolaroo. Not now. That day, when I told Mum about finding the kittens she said yes, they were too sick and too many to stay alive and anyway go outside and play now. When she looked away she had a black cheek and bandages on her hand. She is bright though, my mum, like a moon.

My dad was bright again that night, the kitten night, with the red splotches down his face and Mum all quiet

like she used to go. Scrunched up. Thwacking me, Dad
was, and calling me his little mate. Like with the horses.
They're yer mates, horses. Don't let 'em smell fear give
'em a strong hand and they're mates. Ever seen a horse
being broken? Mad and fierce one minute, then soft and
quiet like a girl, if it's been broken good. Dad was good.
Hard with 'em, like they would know. Who was the strong
one, the not afraid one, they would know that for sure.
Men came from Teralba, Booragul, the Point, all around,
for Dad to break their horses. We had a paddock out the
back and another one over in Teralba. All the horses
round – Teralba, Booragul, Cockle Creek, the Point – they
were all broken by my dad. You could ask anybody, Dad
broke the best. All the sweat slipping on him and the flush
on his face. Blood speckling the mouth where he pulled
on the reins. The bit has to cut in, they have to feel,
it has to gash. For them to know. To know who's boss.
Sometimes they'd foam up and Kari would cry, scream.
Get inside, you stupid bitch – Dad all flushed and forgetting.
Sometimes white would speckle like foam at his mouth
too. That was before. Before, when Kari could scream,
enough to make Dad forget, yell: *Go ON, get frigging well
inside.* The bit gashing the mad stallion. *Mad bloody stallion*,
Dad would say. His mates all laughing going: *Yair, mad
bloody stallion. Carn, ya randy bastard, what about the poor
bloody horse?* Rahah Heh. Sitting on the rails I go: raha heh
randy stallion. Dad's mates slap me on the back till I almost
fall under the hooves: *Teach him early, Mal*, raha heh. My
hands are white in the place I grip the rails, but I am
staring hard at Dad, at not being frightened.

Dad wasn't even frightened in the war. Not even with
the Japs making him walk all that way through the jungle.
Nah. Hated Japs but. Mad stinking bastards, Japs. I
thought Jap was a kind of animal, possibly with claws,
lurking on jungle paths. Like Niggers. Nigger, I thought,

was a kind of water animal on account of catch a nigger by the toe. You catch him going up a creek, I thought, like maybe a platypus. Like you can never catch a platypus. And Dad says you can never catch a nigger.

Ah, anyway, all of this – the horses and backslapping – all this was before. Before Dad was someone we visited and felt strange standing all clean in front of. Scrubbed up and shining we would be. He'd hug Kari, pick her up all careful, like a new bridle. Inspecting, turning her around and around in the air, checking for marks. *G'day, little mate*, to me. And then Kari kissing and kissing him. Dad going, *Ah that's enough now, Blossom, down you go*. All soft he would go, his edges blurring, touching her. Then looking away, sparky and hard man again, my dad. Only yelled at Kari the spastic when he was breaking. Scared she wouldn't know about the horses hoovers and doovers he would say later, all soft, holding her. Scared she would squeal and run under like skipping rope. Couldn't bear it if she were hurt, if she were a squashed Blossom. Going hard at Mum then. *Garn runna bath for yer daughter.*

She ran it too hot once, Kari got in and turned to white and pink and shrieking. Dad pussing mad at Mum across the bath: *You stupid friggin cow, you careless friggin COW*, while the spastic stayed in the bath, pink and screaming. Till Dad remembered and lifted her out like a bit of salted garden slug. Put her down carefully before he knocked Mum for six across the tiles. She didn't say nothing, Mum, just lay there looking at him while the spastic snivelled and I hid behind the clothes basket. Always making trouble she was, that girl, that sister. Couldn't do a thing. Girls are weak chuck 'em in the creek, boys are strong like King Kong.

Boys are strong like King Kong. Me and Bruce Berry, whose mum is Thelma, stomping, stomping like men through the flat. Yelling and flushed up. Using sticks for guns and dressing gown cords for whips. We are the Kings of the castle. Stomp stomp: *Get out, youse kids, I'll give you strong, I'm strong enough to lift the two of youse with one hand before I chuck youse. Get bloody out.* This is fat Thelma, yelling over her fat shoulder. *Fat frigging libber*, I call and run outside, breathless and wild. Like a mad stallion I am.

Bruce Berry has been reading something. Something English. *Let's run away to sea.* Outside, on the lawn, it is possible. We are fierce red pirates, soldiers, sparky hard men we are. The Docks! Bruce Berry is counting money from his pocket, saying: *We'll go to the Docks, jump on a ship, be sailors in the Navy.* Blustery and overloud on the bus, buying tickets from an unsuspecting driver, sitting high on the back seat, making faces at ladies with babies and shopping. I have never before been on a bus alone, but I am no baby. I am a wild sailor of the sea, that's what I am.

The docks are noisy and big. Bigger than my dreams. Bigger than I remembered from the one day, visiting here with Dad. A long time ago that was. I was just a kid, holding Dad's hand, hiding my face on the back of his big palm. Bruce Berry is looking so sick and scared he is like a girl. I almost hold his hand he is such a girl, suddenly all weak. Chuck you in the creek I say. *Wot?* He is called back from somewhere far, still, while the crates of the docks slap and break around him. Hey! I say, hey! We have to find a boat. A fierce red sailor's boat.

The edge of the dock isn't like the edge of the creek or even the lake. It is sudden, a big cement kathwop, ending like a smack in the face. You are walking walking walking, bustled among the noise and then kathwop: a metal stair ladder going up like the beanstalk. Up to the clouds, and up. Joining on to a boat. A big shining blue and white boat. As big as the world. We step back, dizzy, from the edge. Look up to where the boat really truly touches the sky. Way up there, up top, up front, is a flag. Big and flapping away up there. Not like the flag we wave when the Queen comes, or the little ones on a stick we buy at the Easter show. Nicer, this flag – like a picture. White, with a big red circle smack dead in the middle. Nice, I like it.

Then a brown hand, small and hairless, on my shoulder. I look up to a brown face, flat and small like the hand. A voice, not like a big man's voice, saying, *You lost, hey?* No, not lost I say. Sailors. We're looking for a boat. He says: *Runaway, hey?* No, no, I say – like he is stupid or not listening. Sailors. Looking for a boat. A flat white grin crosses his face: *Ah. Ah yes, now I am seeing. A boat, hey? We take you to see a boat – just for a little, mind.* Bruce Berry is looking still more white and bug-eyed. Saying nothing, like a girl.

We follow the brown man up the clanky stairs. Onto the big blue and white boat. Another brown man comes out. They make bird sounds at each other and laugh. The first man touches my shoulder, saying: *Yes, small for a sailor but good, hey?* Laughing. Not like the laughing in the paddock, loud and thwacking, this laughing is soft, invites me in. More brown men, like bugs under summer stones, running running running. And all jabbering like birds, quick and high cacking clicking at each other. It's a language. Like Spanich. Which I know Spanich because Johnny O'Keefe did 'Everybody Loves Saturday Night' in Spanich once and I could sing the whole thing with the record. Dad said it was just like the real one. Senorita sin sinitty sin, hey-ey, senorita, senorita. Well, this – the birding, the clicking – is just like that. Like Spanich, but not. I tell Bruce: they're like Spanich. We sit in the engine room, hot, smelly and noise-filled, drinking sweet green cordial and swinging our legs. Being invited into the soft laughing. Are you like Spanich? I say to the brown man, my legs bashing against the wall. Soft laugh. *No*, he says, *not Spanich. Japanese.* Something slides in my head. Japanese. Click. Is that like Jap? I say. His eyes go wide, startled. *Yes. yes, Jap, hey. I guess so, I guess Jap*, hyeh hyeh. Inside my stomach everything has just gone black and thick and tumbly. My lips feel glugged up like early morning eyes, thick with sleep. I spill my cordial on the wide white trousers of the Jap sailor as I run, grabbing Bruce Berry's hand, not even caring then if it is being like a girl. They would take us to the jungle on this boat, burn us and starve us. I saw a photo of Dad once, in the button box. Short handsome hair, like now, but shoulders sticking out and bones poking through his front. Squinting, like Kari does. Stupid. How stupid could I be? The brown man behind me calling: *Sorry? Hokay boy? Boy hokay?* Clattering on the metal stairs, Bruce Berry puffing hard, but not me boy, I am just running like a man.

In among the legs on the dock we smack crash into some blue police legs. *Lost, mate?* A proper man's voice, gruff like Dad. Yes, I say this time: yes, lost. Trembling, that the Japs might follow us, find us, steal us away to the jungle. Yes, lost. *Know yer address, mate?* Before I remember, I am saying: we own the Police Station in Boolaroo. That's where I live. Forgetting that I don't, not any more. Mal Spence's boy, I say, that's who I am. Because I have not forgotten that, who I am.

They take us to the station in a Highway Patrol car, Bruce Berry all flushed because of the fast. Not me though, I've been in these cars speeding fast lots of times. Anyway, I am busy with the sick in my stomach.

In the station, I sit on the bench in front of Dad. Tell that I ran away, tell that I looked at the boats, tell that I got lost. And can I come and live with him again? *No*, he says, his face hard and looking away, and: *Where's your sister?* The mad sick in my stomach bunches up tight, then catapults out with: I was on a Jap boat, they gave me green drink and made me laugh and I liked them and I want to go and live with them. With the Japs.

Dad pushes both of us, me and Bruce Berry, into the car – the Holden, not the wagon – and we drive and drive with no words not even one.

At the flat, Bruce Berry runs to fat Thelma, hides under her arm. Mum gets up and fast-walks to her room, with Kari. Weak spastic head. The bedroom door slams shut behind Dad and I hear Mum screaming and screaming and Kari yelling: *Get off get off off off off you poofter.* Her callipers clinking as she runs across the room, calling at him: *Stop get off.* Then a big sound of her scream and a thud like a tree against the wall. Her screaming stops then.

The silence echoes round my head all night.

RAISE A GLASS
TO MR SING

Jonathan Falla

As Mal stepped travel-sick off the bus in Fang, the steady rain made his depression run, so that it washed and bled in dark streaks from his head down every other part of him, and his gangling legs moved in an indeterminate, waterlogged sort of way. Nor was his elongated, puttyish face improved by rain. He shrugged his green kitbag higher onto his shoulder as the Thai rickshaw boys began to tug at it from under the plastic sacks they held over their heads. He was a foot taller than the boys, and their grins and wheedling irritated and aggravated his despondency. He pushed through them all, putting his shoe straight into a stream of grey effluent from the market behind the buses. He steered for an open-fronted café opposite.

He was cold, and his thin cotton jacket wasn't helping. He wanted a lodging, he wanted a room in which he could put on every stitch he had. He called, 'Coffee?' at the waiters in the loudly questioning tone of Europeans who are not confident that Thais have ever heard of coffee, lit a cigarette for its puny comfort, and pulled out his budget guidebook to see if Fang's flophouses were listed. It was too bad she hadn't turned up for the bus, just too bad. Was he to book in single or double? Doubtless he was spinning himself a sad fantasy, to imagine that she might materialize off the next bus – but couldn't he just feel her warm belly under a rough blanket. The coffee came in a white glass cup; he loaded it with sugar and thrashed about in the doldrums. He was lonely, he was sick of his own thoughts. He heard a little inner voice snicker that he had thought himself an independent spirit. He wished to God that she'd come, but why had he believed for one second that she might? He dearly wished that the rain would stop.

He needed company, did Mal; his self-pity cranked up his loneliness. When a plastic wallet of photographs was placed by his coffee cup, he regarded it with pre-emptive dislike and a voice leaden with discouragement.

'What's this?'

He looked up. A stocky, middle-aged Thai-Chinese wearing a blue shirt and blue shorts, blue plastic flip-flops and a cream straw trilby stood by Mal's table, beaming at him.

'I am Mr Sing,' began the newcomer, deftly flicking the little wallet open, 'and these are all my friends . . .' In each clear pocket was portrayed a tourist, invariably young, standing alongside the gentleman in blue. To Mal they looked offensively happy.

'You come on the bus,' continued this Mr Sing, 'and I like to invite you –'

'I'm not in the market,' said Mal.

Mr Sing could see that, because the market was on the far side of the road.

Encouraged, he continued: 'I like to suggest a tour of interesting –'

'What's more,' said Mal, standing, 'I'm expecting a friend.'

'Oh, very nice,' smiled Mr Sing.

Mal's chair juddered loudly aside as he lifted his bag. He moved directly to the wooden steps and out onto the liquid streets of Fang.

'No rain tomorrow!' called Mr Sing, behind him. Mal stepped outside, wondering whether to buy a cheap umbrella, uncomfortably realizing that he hadn't located Fang in the guidebook and still didn't know . . .

'Sukothai Guesthouse!' the man called once more.

Mal glanced round and saw Mr Sing laughing cheerfully, waving him towards the side street opposite. He looked down the side street; a sign projected from a wooden frontage, saying *Sukothai Guesthouse*. A burst of thunder; the rain grew heavier.

He'd have to come out eventually, thought Mr Sing. He'd have to eat. That dismal expression: that would mean hunger, wouldn't it? Mr Sing could never quite tell with foreigners. When the six o'clock bus failed to produce anyone else of interest, Mr Sing remained in the vicinity, passing the time of day with acquaintances in the market. In the two years since he had lost his job he had learned persistence, battling to support Neri and the babies, to salvage something from the disgrace of drink – and to stave off the landlord, whose hints were hardening into demands. Mr Sing's cheerfulness was forced; eviction, humiliation and catastrophe loomed. What was he to do: take his family to some muddy, malarial village, build a bamboo hut and be a farmer? He could as easily fly.

The rain had slowed to an inoffensive sinking mist, blending not unpleasantly with smoke of wood and charcoal. The little town was coming to life for the evening. Shortly thereafter, Mr Sing saw the lanky, washed-out Mal reappear from Sukothai Guesthouse and return directly to the coffee shop, sitting at a table deeper in the shadow and reaching brusquely for the menu. Mr Sing studied the long face from just outside – but could read nothing in it.

He gave Mal time to start eating, so that he couldn't

run away, so that he'd be warmer and less irritable. The
boy had ordered the shop's one foreign dish, a tinned
'American burger'. Then, instead of the photographs, Mr
Sing took out a battered road map of the vicinity and held
it open like an offering as he approached Mal. The latter's
mouth was full, so he could not be instantly dismissive.
Mr Sing surprised him by saying not a word for a moment,
merely sitting with the map on his knee and smiling
politely, letting Mal chew his gristly meat. And then:

'I like to propose to you.'

Mal, happier inside but with his guard well up, scrutin-
ized Mr Sing. As hustlers went, he thought, the man was
modest enough. Mal lit another cigarette. Mr Sing laid
out his map on the table. A number of locations in the
orbit of Fang were marked in red ballpoint.

'One day touring by motorcycle with Mr Sing, to lovely
and interesting places; we can see Akha hill tribe, we can
see old China Army, we can see Good For Democracy.'

'What's that?' asked Mal, struggling not to sound
interested. This was not difficult; since puberty, Mal's lugubrious Black Country accent and sebaceous face had amal-
gamated with all the sparkle of lard.

'Ha ha, Mr Sing's surprise! Everybody likes it. You come
with me, one day tomorrow?'

Don't be taken for a ride! said Mal to himself, faintly embarrassed by his own wit. Secretly, however, he was beginning
to be glad of Mr Sing's company. In the hour in which
he had skulked and dried off at Sukothai Guesthouse, Mal
had forced himself to acknowledge that Cathy (or had it
been Kath?) would not be coming. He had toyed with the
idea of returning to Bangkok, or Chiang Mai or anywhere
but this backwater he'd manoeuvred himself into. He
could meet people in Chiang Mai! But then, with that
excruciating pseudo-scrutiny of the self-pitying, he had
lamented, *You could meet ten thousand people right here, but*

you won't. His fledgling and contradictory resolves had died. He only knew that to turn tail from Fang by return of bus would be mortifying. He knew that he'd stay a day at least. So what was he going to do?

He peered some more at Mr Sing. The middle-aged man's eyes twinkled engagingly. He carried a row of ballpoints of several colours in his breast pocket. There was something oddly trustworthy about the ballpoints.

'It would have to be jolly interesting,' he said, with dark emphasis.

Jolly? Mr Sing believed he knew the word. The dismal face in front of him seemed anything but jolly – or was he wrong? How could you make out anything in such dank, pale features? He gazed at Mal's long countenance; could he not somehow win the boy's custom? And then be able to pay off the landlord? Oh, it was worth a try!

'It will be a jolly day. Mr Sing guarantees!'

Jolly?

Mal sucked on his cigarette, and stared back at him. In desperation, Mr Sing tried one last throw.

'You don't enjoy, you don't pay!'

Mal nodded.

'Where'd you learn English?' called Mal over Mr Sing's shoulder as, in bright morning sunlight, they sped away from town on a little blue scooter. He clung to the rear edge of the seat. He'd never actually ridden pillion on a bike before, but was buggered if he'd show nerves.'

'I am professional man,' replied Mr Sing. 'Former assistant pharmacist.'

'What happened?' shouted Mal.

'What?'

'You didn't give up pharmacy to do motorbike tours – so what happened?'

Mr Sing did not at once reply. It occurred again to Mal (as it had done so painfully the evening before while the rain had roared upon the roof of Sukothai Guesthouse) that there could be reasons for his own lack of a large circle of friends.

At last, Mr Sing offered: 'In pharmacy is going nowhere. I look for B-52.'

They swerved violently to avoid a bullock cart laden with three-metre bamboos, and hit a pothole which banged the suspension hard. Mr Sing clucked with annoyance and Mal winced, trying to get a grip on what he had heard.

'How do you mean, B-52? Like the bomber?'

'Very good airplane! Very powerful, flies a long way. Like a good job. Mrs Thatcher had a B-52, but she has crashed, ha ha!'

He hooted with laughter, and the bike lurched danger-ously. Mal thought of a joke about Mrs Thatcher's destruc-tive capacity, but he wasn't going to risk laughing with Mr Sing: it might distract or encourage him, and the ride was unnerving already. Mr Sing noted Mal's silence with disappointment. Mrs Thatcher's B-52 had usually been a surefire chuckler with the English – which (so his diction-ary had confirmed) was what *jolly* was all about. He'd give Mal *jolly* if it killed them both. A shame the bike was so pitifully small; the boy must find it a sorry sort of thrill. He opened the throttle wide.

They whirred on alongside a line of low hills, through the lurid green of maturing paddy. They wobbled amongst slow country rickshaws carrying hundredweights of veg-etables, young girls walking with banana leaves wrapped around cakes for Fang market on their heads, and farmers pushing bicycles with travel-sick chickens slung upside down from the crossbars. They dodged noisome trucks which seemed disposed to hurl Mal and Mr Sing into the ditch in a heap of blood, metal and sharp fractured plastic.

Many of the trucks were laden with a teetering mass of people.

'Where are they all heading?' called Mal, attempting to pitch his voice deeper for sober effect.

'Maybe refugee,' shouted Mr Sing. 'Burma people, Laos people. Thailand more jolly for them.' He was getting to like that word.

To Mal's horror, the guide turned his face right round to look at him. Trucks and rickshaws and pigs on strings came at them in a lethal flood and Mr Sing was facing backwards, grinning! In an instant, the blood drained from Mal's face. 'The boy is not jolly at all,' said Mr Sing to himself. 'What to do?'

Worried by this, he swerved past an oncoming lorry laden with cement, then began to sing Thai romantic hits, loud and strong. As his feeling for the music swelled, so Mr Sing's hands came off the handlebars to conduct the balmy air.

Mal waited for both hands to rise together: *then* he'd protest!

Just then, however, Mr Sing turned off the highway onto a gravel road. After half a mile they reached the foot of the hills and began to climb. Mal was uncertain which to be more thankful for: the panorama of forested peaks, thatched villages steaming in the sun and hill streams that glittered in the clear blue morning, or the fact that, uphill on dirt, the little scooter could manage barely ten miles an hour in first gear.

It became cooler. They climbed higher still.

'Where are we going?' asked Mal.

'Old China Army,' said Mr Sing.

The bike slithered alarmingly on the now greasy red track. In fright, Mal stabbed uselessly at the ground with his metre-long legs, remembered the 'No fun, no pay' clause, and wondered how early in the day he could claim.

94

They reached a saddle in the low ridge. As they crossed the watershed, the landscape turned markedly bleaker. Mr Sing stopped to point. Beneath them was an artificial lake, a reservoir surrounded by hills long since stripped of trees and left to scraggy saplings and elephant grass. By the lake was a village of muddy roadways and huts of rough-sawn timber that looked old and dark, and probably teemed with scorpions and cockroaches. In the centre of the village was a flagpole, and the flag was red and blue with a large white sun in the corner. Mal gazed at it – and thought he had strayed into an old movie.

'What's all this?' he wondered.

'Old China Army. Kuomintang still like to fight Mr Mao.'

'KMT!' mused Mal. 'The bloody Nats!'

'You shall visit. Very nice place for you.'

As they came down the track into the village, the leathery faces of elderly Chinese exiles glanced up without expression. They'd been here thirty-five years and a good few foreigners had passed through, some with suggestions for the overthrow of Communism, others just to gawp. Mr Sing was familiar; a regular, usually with a tourist up behind.

Mr Sing stopped the scooter outside the village shop. Mal got off with relief. He stood peering about him, vaguely fingering his camera but not lifting it.

'Odd,' he said. 'What do they do all day?'

'Prepare to conquer China,' whispered his companion. 'KMT very old, all dying now.'

Mal gazed in fascination. It was weird, it was intriguing; a lost army in the hills!

'Too much,' he said, in his usual flat voice.

Mr Sing studied him anxiously. Too much? Too much what? Didn't he think the Kuomintang jolly at all? It was the jolliest bit of militarism in the neighbourhood and tourists generally loved it. He felt a twinge of anxiety: what if the whole trip was a joyless disaster and the boy refused to pay?

He went purposefully to the open wooden flap of the shop, where sachets of detergent hung in long tails above the torch batteries and sweets. Mr Sing muttered to the girl, then called to Mal, 'Oh, yes please!'

Two scratched tumblers of clear fluid were passed out. Mal wrinkled his nose and sipped: 'Jesus!' His top lip stung, his tongue shrivelled and the sting made his eyes water.

Mr Sing took command. 'You drink like DC-3, sip sip slow. I teach you F-15!' He threw the contents of the tumbler down his throat. 'OK, jolly yes?'

Mal, eyes still moist, thought of the alcohol hitting Mr Sing's faculties of co-ordination and regarded his driver glumly. Mr Sing's anxiety redoubled. The boy looked miserable. He didn't like the rum: the KMT hadn't hit the jolly note at all: get him out of here. He dropped a coin in the tin, cried, 'Akha now! Akha!' and pulled Mal towards the scooter.

They puttered off as fast as the little machine would go. Mal gazed back at the geriatric Chinese brigade. He wished he'd got himself together to ask questions before being bustled away.

Akha's jolly as hell, thought Mr Sing resolutely. Akha's primitive. They slithered up the track. He was bloody well going to get a smile out of Mal; he was beginning to consider it a mission. He gave the morning another round of Thai popular love songs. Occasionally, foreigners responded to these in kind. Not Mal; he was intent on Mr Sing's grip on the handlebars, alert for signs of intoxication. Song or no song, he could see that the guide was struggling on the dreadful road. He was not a young man.

They turned a corner. Mr Sing pointed and announced again, 'Akha!' – but before Mal could comprehend, they hit a deep muddy rut and fell off. The bike's tiny motor shrilled and raced a moment, the back wheel spinning. Mal staggered aside cursing with his ankle scraped. Mr Sing picked himself up and heaved at the scooter, puffing with effort. He knocked a lump of reddish mud from the handlebar grip, then wiped his sweating forehead, leaving it streaked gritty red. He called wheezily, 'Sorry, sorry. That is Akha, where there is swinging!'

Mal was about to say that steering was the immediate problem when he realized that they'd reached the edge of a village. The Akha tribal settlement sat on a treeless ridge above the forested hills. Children mooched and played among the large, dark thatched houses that were long and low, ancient and concealing. Small women pounded rice and spun yarn, dressed in embroidered black tunics and leggings that would have made them look like public schoolboys were it not for the silver-hung headdresses piled on top. Mal was twice the women's height. The gossips, sucking on their home-rolled cigarettes, eyed his absurd length of sandy-haired leg with mild distaste but grinned cheerfully. A profusion of craven dogs skulked in dust holes.

'We take our lunch,' announced Mr Sing.

Here, the shop stood at the edge of the village overlooking the houses. Outside, rough wooden benches crowded a small table. The owner wore none of the black garb, Mal saw: perhaps he wasn't Akha, perhaps he was Thai or Chinese or mongrel; perhaps he was a modernist Akha dressed for trade. It was all rather odd. Mal puzzled at it with a frown of curiosity.

His guide noted only the frown: *the boy was bored!*

'Swinging, swinging!' yelped Mr Sing, his voice shrill. 'Girls are swinging there!'

He pointed. On a spur over a steep slope of scrub stood a pyramid framework, three spindly poles lashed together at the top. A rope hung in the centre with a loop at the end. There was no one anywhere near it.

'Not today,' said Mr Sing. 'One-a-year ceremony swing.'

Mal looked round searchingly; he liked to hear about weird ceremonies. 'Bit rum,' he said.

Mr Sing stared at him in surprise – then hurriedly snapped his fingers at the proprietor and gave an order. There was a rattling in the back of the shop and, a moment later, a single scratched glass of spirits was on the table. Mal raised an eyebrow, looking in concern at Mr Sing. They'd fall off again for sure!

'For you,' said the guide. 'With compliments.'

So relieved was Mal that Mr Sing was abstaining, that he picked up and drank generously of the firewater. Then a second glass, just washed and filled, was passed out to Mr Sing. As Mal stared, his driver tossed it down and laughed: 'One more F-15, all right!'

Mal would now have despaired of his life – had not the rum begun to restore his morale. It was crude stuff, but it was certainly warming. He told himself that there were times when one just had to go with the flow. The spirits jangled his stomach lining. He saw the smoke of cooking fires rising through the thatch of the village houses.

'Did you say lunch?'

'Coming,' said Mr Sing.

'Traditional, is it?' continued Mal, settling back and regarding the rope swing.

This was unfair, thought Mr Sing; the boy was all contradictions. How to know what he'd like? He seemed displeased by everything, then called for more. He'd wept over KMT rum, but wanted Akha rum. He'd consumed a disgusting 'American burger' in Fang, and now he was demanding traditional food. Akha food! One taste of that and the day was doomed. If he agreed to pay for the tour at all, he would doubtless haggle over the price, refuse to tip and write something awful in the comments book. Filled with doubts, Mr Sing changed the order.

A plate of stewed meat and rice arrived.

'For you,' smiled Mr Sing, who wouldn't have eaten Akha food for the world. 'Very traditional, very good!'

Mal tucked in hungrily. 'What is it?' he asked.

Unhappily, Mr Sing nodded towards a dog sleeping by the house post nearby. A man was strolling towards the dog, his hands clasped casually behind his back.

'Beef?' said Mal, 'Buffal—'

Without warning, the man produced a wooden cudgel and brought it down onto the dog's skull with a wet thud. The blow was crushing. The animal's head, slightly flattened, was pushed out over the dirt. The lips curled in slow spasm, blood spurting from the nose.

Mal froze, his spoon at his mouth. The man stooped and grabbed the dog by its tail, hoiking it towards the kitchen at the rear of the thatched house next door. Mr Sing tried to sound urbanely informative.

'Must be silent. If dog is barking just a little bit, flavour is gone.'

Mal put down the spoon slowly.

'This is my idea!' said Mr Sing frantically. 'Here they sell eggs. We take them to Geneva!'

With a bag of four raw eggs in Mal's pocket and a large Pepsi bottle of rum plugged with paper in Mr Sing's pouch, the bike wobbled its way along the ridge. They dropped into a humid valley, crossed a slimy wooden bridge, turned up a side track through lusher vegetation – and all at once were confronted by clouds of steam rising from a forest pool. On the far side of the pool stood massive arrangements of steel pipes and monstrous valves, curled and bolted and stuck into the ground by a concrete shed with a strongly padlocked door.

'Geneva,' announced Mr Sing.

'Says *Geothermal*,' said Mal, studying a signboard.

Mr Sing was wearing a fixed smile. This was one of his interesting jokes, and it was time Mal gave him his due. He insisted:

'Geneva! Very big negotiations right here.'

'Now what?' speculated Mal. 'Don't tell me . . .'

So Mr Sing didn't tell him, and felt near to tears. Mal looked at him expectantly.

'So? Who's negotiating?'

He doesn't want to know, then he does want to know! Mr Sing thought of his landlord and the sorely needed fee that seemed to mock and recede from his grasp – and he kept up the fixed smile.

'Thailand Army, Burma Army,' he said.

'Border security?' asked Mal, with an enjoyable frisson of fear.

Mr Sing replied: 'No, no, shareout for opium smugglers. You have the eggs?'

Blinking, Mal handed over the bag and wondered what Mr Sing would spring on him next. Mr Sing delved in his pouch and brought out a length of pink plastic twine. He attached this to opposite rims of his straw trilby, placed the eggs inside and lowered them into the near-boiling pool. He crooned another song the while. A genial picture, thought Mal.

They ate the hard-boiled eggs sitting on a colossal valve. Mr Sing pulled the bottle of liquor from his pouch, whipped out the paper plug and passed it over. They both began to pull steadily at it, watching the pond that bubbled in a tranquil, musical way.

Mr Sing blurted out, 'A nice song of love by a forest pool!' and sang again, his spirited gestures disguising glances at Mal. The lugubrious youth was waving the bottle, nodding slightly. How bizarre he was! He seemed to have no interest in war, or tribal colour, or weird food or any of Mr Sing's jokes – but show him hot mud and he nodded. Mr Sing gave up trying to understand, and sang on.

Something caught Mal's eye. He stood, and wobbled a few paces to where muddy pockets heaved and slopped as steam popped up. The noise was thick and ridiculous. To Mal's increasingly uninhibited imagination, it suggested only one thing: 'Sounds like diarrhoea,' he said to himself.

Slowly, a puerile grin seeped into the corners of Mal's fleshly lips. *Oh, is he jolly?* thought Mr Sing.

'Mud, mud, glorious mud,' Mal hiccupped. Mr Sing stared at him.

'It is a song?'

'Song about mud,' shrugged Mal, sucking at the bottle.

'Sing!' cried Mr Sing.

As though a chock had been pulled away, Mal lifted his head and began tunelessly:

'Mud, mud, shitty old mud,
Nothing quite like it for heating the blood.
So follow me, follow, down to the hollow,
And there we will wallow in boiling diarrhoea.'

'Oh!' Mr Sing beat his hands together in rapture. The day might be saved and the landlord paid even yet.

'I tell you,' he confided, 'it is time for Good For Democracy. Mr Sing's special!'

To his joy, Mal beamed back at him, the soul of jollity.

They came, without toppling off, to another village. They were high up now, but Mal could not tell whether it was cloud or mist that swirled about them and what was the difference anyway? He had begun to feel cold again. The mountain valley was close and thickly forested. The trees had silver-grey trunks and olive-green leaves that glistened with condensation. A slight drizzle began. Mal *was* cold.

They stopped before the first house, where the track decayed into rivulets and mud slides. Between heavy, dripping foliage that arched over the pathways, Mal saw the huts. They were small and mean, with none of the grandeur of the Akha village. These had a timorous, furtive look. Thin stilts propped up the floors and walls of flattened bamboo, the thatch was black, balding and bedraggled, and growing weeds. Several were listing badly as their supports rotted. Vines and creepers swarmed over them.

'Lisu tribe village,' said Mr Sing. It seemed deserted, almost abandoned. Mr Sing pointed at a house some thirty yards from the road, said, 'Good For Democracy!' brightly and pushed his way through saturated fronds towards it. Mal followed.

There was no one in sight, but his guide seemed confident, walking straight to the front door up a sloping timber ramp that to Mal looked slippery and rotten. He beckoned Mal to come, then pushed open the door.

When new, the interior would have been quite dark; now there was patchy light, because large holes had appeared in the roof and walls. The fire was so dead that a black cat lay asleep in the ashes. Household clutter hung from the walls: old baskets with their handles coming loose, a plastic mug, a torn fishing net, plenty of rags. The place was littered with tin cans, the labels burned off. Mal could see no one – until a slight stir drew his eye to a woman sitting in deep shadow, her back to the wall. She was chewing joylessly on a piece of roasted corn. She looked to be in her worn and haggard thirties, her T-shirt shapeless and her sarong without meaningful colour. Then Mal saw the rest of the family, four in all, lying on faded plastic mats and perfectly still.

The woman gazed vacantly at Mr Sing, who raised a cheery hand in greeting.

He turned to Mal and said: 'You want Good For Democracy?'

The phrase acted like a trigger. The woman nudged the nearest male and of a sudden the whole family was awake. They pulled the mats to the centre of the floor and from the shadows brought a small, filthy pillow. The man lit two candles in glass jars, and scraped some brown gunk onto a screwtop lid. Someone was rummaging in a cloth bag that hung from a nail. They said nothing, not to Mr Sing, nor Mal, nor each other, but watched Mal closely. They looked as decrepit as their home, their arms and legs wasted, the skin loose on their bones. They looked as though this burst of energy would finish them. It was perhaps their one moment of activity all week. It felt, thought Mal, quite desperate.

Mr Sing was grinning at him again, but the grin was forced, not jolly. The woman was heating the brown gunk over a candle flame and a sickly reek of opium began. Mal saw the brass pipe and thought, I'm supposed to lie down with these addicts.

'Yes, Good For Democracy,' leered Mr Sing, 'make for understanding with all peoples.'

Mal understood only that he wanted none of it.

'I think not,' he said. Mr Sing's fixed smile wavered.

'Not?'

'Not.'

'Not good?'

'Not for me. Not good for me.'

He turned, pushed at the decaying bamboo door and went out.

They rode back to Fang, chilled and silent. At the tea-shop, Mal got off the scooter and watched Mr Sing pull the muddy little machine onto its stand. The guide was exhausted. He was wet, he looked old, his eyes were dulled. He had been driving all day with no more protection than rice spirit. Suddenly, Mal felt embarrassed and sorry.

'Listen,' he said, 'we both need a hot drink.'

For a moment Mr Sing hesitated: it was he who should be making the running, leading the day. But his resistance was short-lived. Mal ordered hot Milo. Still they said little. Mr Sing seemed to be wanting to speak, but the rejection of Democracy had been a profound shock. A defeat.

Mal pulled cash from his shirt pocket and put the tour price on the table. For a moment, Mr Sing showed no reaction. He stared at the money so sadly that, on an impulse, Mal added another note. Mr Sing glanced up, surprised.

'Oh, thank you.'

'Look,' said Mal, as emphatically as he could, 'I have to say that it really was jolly interesting. All of it, jolly interesting.'

'Yes?' Mr Sing seemed very uncertain.

'Absolutely.'

At last, the weary face broke into a smile of gratitude. 'Oh yes?'

'Yes, really,' insisted Mal.

As though only now finding the courage, Mr Sing opened his little pouch and brought out a green exercise book covered in plastic film. There was a photograph of himself and the scooter taped to the front, and *Mr Sing's Tours* in large red ballpoint letters. He opened it.

'You will write for me?'

Page on page of testimonials in English and Dutch, French and German. Brief or verbose, everyone had had a jolly time with Mr Sing. Unprepared, Mal stared at the blank page in front of him. Mr Sing watched: he wasn't going to refuse now, was he?

Then Mal picked up the pen and wrote, *Raise a glass to Mr Sing*.

The guide pulled the book across the table, peering at the curious phrase.

'Not bad for me?' he asked.

'No, not bad,' said Mal.

'Thank you, too much,' smiled Mr Sing.

He picked up his hot Milo, relief flooding his tired face, his B-52 at long last cleared for take-off.

MISSING PHOTOGRAPHS

Michel Faber

The points of the dressmaking shears tremble violently an inch away from his neck. She can't hold them still; her rage and the weight of the metal are too heavy. She lays him down beside her on the bed and puts the shears back into her knitting basket, slipping her fingers instead through the tiny silver scissors she uses for cutting her nails. These weigh nothing and hug her fingers like jewellery, as much a part of her as her wedding ring. With a whisper of lubricated metal she parts the blades and jabs one point through his chest, just under the collar; there is a moment of resistance, then the blade slides in right up to the crux. She begins to scissor, cutting across his neck from ear to ear. The tension in her limbs, of which she has scarcely been aware until now, peaks and ebbs away: the basic act is done: the rest is finishing touches. She must be careful not to cut into the bricks of the house behind him, for the house is blameless and worth remembering. There is a brass plaque behind his left shoulder, too, with a partially obscured inscription on it: she might want to guess at that inscription again one day in the future, and she'll need every letter then. She snips carefully, manoeuvring close to the crux, following every contour of his body along the outer edges. At last he falls out of the picture and lands noiselessly in her lap. The photograph of her first wedding party now has a perfect husband-shaped hole in place of the groom. She reinserts the picture into its tabs in the album; he is no longer standing at her side. She picks up the next photograph on the pile, and immediately punctures his smiling mouth, ripping a furrow all the way up through his brow. Behind him, a garden hedge glistens after a summer shower in 1952. Not one leaf of it is she prepared to sacrifice.

When she is finished, her lap is full of little mutilated images of him, most of them black and white, one or two of them colour, all of them so very small. Cutting them out has given her a headache: eyestrain. She gathers them up in one hand and tosses them, scrunched by a single convulsive squeeze, into the waste-paper basket, then folds the photo album shut. Her nightdress is damp with perspiration. It is New Year's Eve 1959, and facing 1960 is at last a possibility.

Of course, I wasn't there, so I'm just guessing. Picturing. This incident from my mother's life, never recounted by her, is a blank which I fill in with the Polaroid chemicals of my imagination. My mother never tells me anything, so what choice have I got but to resort to this trick photography?

It all started a few weeks ago, when I received a letter from a stranger. The name and address on the back of the envelope were unknown to me; the postage stamps identified it as coming from Poland, the country of my parents' birth. Inside, I found a couple of photographs enfolded by the letter, and of course I examined these first. Has anyone ever received a letter with photographs and read the letter first? I refuse to believe it.

In the first photograph, a blonde woman wearing a knitted pullover with a reindeer pattern on the breast was posing with skis. The skis weren't on her feet but held in one hand, balanced on the ground like a spear. Bright sunshine permitted a shutter speed fast enough to freeze the cloud of breath coming from her lips. I had no idea who this woman might be.

The other photograph depicted her indoors, at closer range. She was perhaps my age, or a couple of years older, with two children and a man with a moustache arranged around her. Frost opaqued the window of her cluttered sitting room, but she wore the thin blouse and knee-length skirt which bespoke central heating and double glazing. On the back of this picture, four names were written in the empty places where the heads would have been if I had X-ray vision. Each name was unknown to me, including '*me*'.

> *Dear Relation,* [the letter said]
>
> *It sorrows me I do not know your name, or what is it you are, is it cousin or however. You must excuse me my language – I learned many years ago English, and have dictionary from antiquated time. I find out from relation of your mother, that your home is in house that your mother lives in many years ago. I know this adres so I am abled to write to you. Your mother does not wish for me to write to her so that is reason I have not write in more youthful times.*
>
> *I am dauhgter of Wojtek Ciebula, husband of your mother before she got different husband what is your father. My father and your mother wished no longer to be in marriage and they gone out of each other in 1958. Then my father meeted a different woman what was my mother in 1959. My name is Anka (Anna) and I am 35 years old technicalwoman in hospital. My husband also is 35 years old telecommunications-engineer, his name is Piotr Kwiatkowski so I am Kwiatkowska also. We live 3 kilometer to Gdansk border, about 20 kilometer to citycenter. We have nice small house with forest up its behind, two children Zola (6) and Marek (8). Also dog that is old and full of love.*

You think perhaps why is this interesting? It sorrows me I cannot break languagebarrier, I must tell you reason for my letter like a customer in a shop telling what is it she wish to buy. I wish for duplicates of photographs of my father Wojtek Ciebula. He was gone out of my mother when I was badly three years, in 1962. She speaked not very frequently over him after this happening, and now she is died. I have no photograph of Wojtek Ciebula from marriagetime, before marriagetime, old man, baby, nothing. Relation of your mother thinks that your mother has photographs of him with certainty. I ask you to possess this photographs away from her for a short time only and make duplicates for me. It sorrows me that I believe your mother wishes not to help me, so you must maybe a different reason give why you the photographs are wishing. Please understand this is not trifle for me, I have great and heartful need for your helping.

Yours faithfully,
Anka Kwiatkowska

Now, I must confess to you that I'm a man with a horror of disappointing people. It's a legacy from my childhood, I guess. If my mother ever said, or even implied, that she wanted me to do something, and I didn't do it, I always got the feeling she skipped a few days forward in her progress towards death. If I toed the line (though often I had no idea what the line *was*) she would live out her life at the normal, even rate. For this reason, it was a relief to me when she moved into a home unit after my father died, and left the house to me. Not that I got any pleasure from inheriting it as real estate, you understand (well, maybe a little, but is that such a bad thing?) – it was more that at last I could do a few things that maybe she wouldn't approve of, without feeling that she'd develop bone cancer or a brain tumour or something. The thing is, I tend to feel more responsible than I should for *other* people as well, so my brave new life as a free spirit hasn't exactly been a spectacular success so far. Getting slightly drunk on a few cans of beer bought in a supermarket five miles further away from me than the local one where all the checkout girls know me is about the extent of it. If there's more to independence, no one's told me what it is yet.

Anyway, I went to visit my mother, burdened with my secret mission. While she was in the kitchen fetching the coffee and cake, I loitered around the modular wooden shelves and cupboards my father had built for her, as if I might sense the photograph albums' location somehow. (I keep having this fantasy, ever since I was a kid, that I've got X-ray vision. On a rational level I know very well I can't see through barriers; I just *wish* I could.)

Instead, I had to raise the subject, man to mother.

'You know, I've been thinking about our . . . ah . . . heritage,' I said.

'Heritage? What heritage?' she wanted to know.

'Our family,' I said.

'You mean *my* family?' she said, squinting through her thick glasses at me.

'Well, yes,' I conceded.

'What about them?'

'Well . . . I've been wondering what would happen if I ever had children, and they wanted to know my history.'

'Children?' she grimaced. 'You're not even married.'

'No, but I may be one day.'

'I'd be surprised if I lived to see it.'

'Well, that's sort of part of what I'm trying to say,' I pressed on, blushing. 'If I had children, and you weren't here any more, and they wanted to know what people in my family – in the past – had looked like . . .'

My mother shrugged and poured more tea.

'I thought you had piles of photographs,' she said, as if she had caught me out losing my pencil-case or my athletics shorts through carelessness again.

'I do,' I assured her, 'but they're all from after I came into the picture. I was thinking of before then.'

'What's to think about before then?'

'I just wouldn't want all that history to get lost, that's all.'

'Lost? How would it get lost?'

'Well . . . just supposing . . .'

Losing patience, my mother rolled her eyes up to heaven.

'If thieves break into this place, do you think they're going to leave the TV and take photograph albums instead?'

'There might be a fire . . .' I suggested.

She clapped a wrinkled palm to her wrinkled forehead.

'Huh! Do you want to give me nightmares of dying in a fire?'

I could see I was getting nowhere, a place my mother had taken me many times before. Clearly, there was nothing for it but the perilous sin of frankness.

'I just think you should let me make some copies of your photographs.'

'Copies?' She was incredulous, as if I had announced my plan to have her photographs cast in bronze.

'Yes, I can get copies made,' I persisted. 'Duplicates, you know. You keep the originals, I keep the copies.'

'Which photographs have you got in mind?' she enquired suspiciously.

'All of them,' I shrugged indulgently. 'It would probably be wrong to have any sort of preconceived idea of which ones were the important ones. You never know what's going to end up being important, do you?'

There was a pause while my mother turned my likely motives over and over in her mind.

'You want to pay,' she summarized at last, 'to get copies of pictures of your father's buddies from the football team back in Lodz?'

'Sure,' I grinned unhappily. 'Why not?'

She stared a bit longer, then slumped a little, as if weakened. Old age had made her a less formidable judge that she'd once been.

'All right,' she said. 'Give me a while to gather things together.'

Two weeks later, after a reminder, my mother handed me four fat photo albums which, when I got them back home, proved indeed to be full of snaps of my father's football buddies back in Lodz. They also contained many pictures of him and my mother, and my mother's mother, and my father's mother, and my mother's sister's husband, and so on and so on. My mother's christening was there, confirmation, first Communion, second wedding.

In a few places, missing photographs had left discoloured rectangles on the page, like ghostly windows. Wojtek Ciebula, if he was anywhere, must have been in those windows.

I wrote to Anka.

> *Dear Anka,*
> *I have asked my mother for her photograph albums and she has lent them to me. There were no photographs of your father*

But no, that wasn't right. Anka's English was so bad, she might think I was trying to claim that no photographs of her father had ever been taken.

. . . *in the albums* I added. But was that quite right, either?

The photographs *had* been in the albums, no doubt, until my mother had removed them. My pen hovered over the page while I mentally tried out a number of additions.

> *because my mother took them out.*
> *I think my mother took them out.*
> *I think my mother may have taken them out.*
> *I think perhaps my mother may have taken them out.*
> *I think perhaps they may have been taken out.*
> *I'm not sure, but I think perhaps*

I took a long frustrated swig of beer. God save Anka from linguistic cowardice and grammatical pussyfooting – her English was bad enough already without this!

> *I don't know what happened to them,* I concluded.

Was that enough? I considered another grab-bag of possibilities.

> *I'm sorry.*
> *These things happen.*
> *Thanks for writing.*
> *If there's anything I can do . . .*
> *It's snowy here too.*
> *The area where you live/your house/your children/your breasts is/are very pretty.*

Christ!

I finished the letter somehow, and posted it. On the same day, I dropped off my mother's photographs at a photo lab for copying. Yes, all of them. You see, I'm terrified of getting caught out lying to my mother. And she can see through me so easily! It would be just like her to ask me for the duplicate of such-and-such a picture, so that she can send it to somebody, or she might simply ask to see the whole lot, to see how they'd come out. So, I took them all in, a big plastic shopping-bag full. It raised the technician's eyebrows, I can tell you. He spelled my name and address very carefully on the order form.

A few weeks later, I returned the albums to my mother, longing to ask what had happened to the photographs of Wojtek.

'Thanks a lot,' I said.

'My pleasure,' she murmured absently. 'Do you want something to eat?'

'Well, no ... er, yes ... but I ...'

'There's not much in the house just now. I don't do the shopping until Friday. Thursday is the day I change the sheets on the bed and do the washing. Saturday is really the best day to come visit me.'

'Well, I don't come for the food, you know.'

She heaved herself out of her chair with a slight groan and walked stiffly towards the kitchen, as if discounting a transparent lie.

'I'll see what I've got in the fridge.'

After a large meal, I broached the subject.

'I've been thinking,' I said.

'More cake? It'll only go stale if you don't eat it. Everything I can get nowadays is in portions too big for one person.'

'I've been wondering,' I struggled on, 'about the photograph albums. There don't seem to be any pictures of your first husband.'

'I threw them away,' she stated flatly as she cleared the table. 'Years ago.'

'Even the ones that had you in them?'

'*Especially* those.'

'You don't regret it?'

'What's to regret?' she demanded, stacking the last dish with a clatter. 'I never look at old photographs anyway. I'm sure people in the old days had no trouble remembering the past without photographs.'

'Yes, but only if they were there at the time.'

'What business is it of people who weren't there?'

I had to follow my mother into the kitchen; she was away.

'Well . . . what about history?' I asked.

She had to laugh.

'History can do without Wojtek Ciebula, I assure you.'

Back home, I tried to imagine how my mother *really* felt.

She looks at her waste-paper bin. It is made of tin. It's the same one she's always had, with stylized peasant boys and girls holding hands all around it like a paper chain. She's never been able to throw that waste bin away, even though it has a few spots of rust on the inside of it now. A hoarder – that's what some people have called her – that woman keeps everything! Ah, but if only she had kept Wojtek. Not Wojtek himself, but at least the pictures. But she threw all the little paper Wojteks into that bin. Superstitiously she checks it in case they might still be lying there, stuck to the bottom maybe, thirty-seven years on. Things like that do happen sometimes. Lolly papers. She checks. Empty.

These days, she has nothing much to put in the waste-paper bin. Everything's been paid off. A plaque on the letterbox threatens legal action to junk mail. Few people write.

Where did all her rubbish go over the years? Is there a city dump where everything piles up, layer upon layer, like in those drawings of geological strata (no photographs then!) in her ancient schoolbooks? Or do they sort the paper rubbish out from the banana peels and the broken toys, and burn it? They must do, they must do, or there would be dumps the size of cities.

Sitting in bed with the mutilated photographs of herself and Wojtek in her lap, she plays with the idea of restoring them in the laboratory of her mind. She peers at the picture of the wedding party outside the old house. All her family are there, impossibly young; even the dead ones are alive again. Only the man next to her is gone, except for . . . His hand on her arm hasn't been cut out, because . . . because why? She can't really remember. Perhaps she didn't want to cut into her own arm. Why was that so important? She knows very well what her own arm looked like, she doesn't need a photo to remind her. So why?

Wojtek's hand is short-fingered, every digit almost the same length. When he held her tight, she would feel the pressure on her back in straight parallel lines – as if she were wearing an old-fashioned peasant dress with a back-lacing bodice that was much too tight, and rows of corded metal eyelets were digging into her.

She tries to remember something else about Wojtek besides the way his hands felt on her back, but she can't. She was married to him for such a short time compared to the years with Peter that there are no physicalities left intact. She imagines a shoulder, a neck, a collarbone: they are all Peter's. She is seeing them as they were, uncovered by the hospital gown when Peter lay dying in the Prince Alfred Hospital. When at last his time came, he dropped away from her as though through a hole in the bed beneath him: she watched him disappear. Where did he go? Nurses took the body away, leaving the bed bare. She stayed in the room, knowing that if Peter still existed somewhere, it had to be somewhere under that bed, or inside it, or above it.

She looks again at the photograph of Wojtek. What? The photograph of . . . ? Yes, that's what it is now. How odd that this photograph of her family has become a photograph of Wojtek. Because he isn't in it.

She holds the picture up to the light. A man-shaped glow

comes through it. The other figures in the picture go dark.

She cut him out so that she could look at the photographs without so much pain. Did she realize then that the mutilation of the pictures would make it impossible for her to show them to anyone else for ever afterwards? Maybe not. Maybe she imagined showing people the pictures and when they pointed at the holes and asked, 'Who was that?' she would say, 'Someone who doesn't deserve to be remembered. And next to him, that's my aunt Kasha, who *blah blah blah* . . .' Maybe she imagined that.

But it couldn't be that way, of course. Her reasons for cutting him out have been reversed somehow. Positive has become negative. She cut him out to stop the sordid secrets of her marriage becoming known to the future. Now it's the mutilated photographs themselves that are the sordid secrets.

Of course, I was just guessing. Again, I wasn't there. Maybe my mother couldn't care less. *I* certainly cared, though. That letter from Anka nagged at me like a brain tumour. (How do I know how a brain tumour nags? Just guessing, again.) I found myself thinking about the way my mother had treated me all through my childhood, and my adolescence, and now. The way I had always been kept in the dark about everything, punished without explanation, judged without forgiveness. And after all these years I still didn't know what, if anything, I had done wrong.

I started to write a long, rambling letter to Anka about these things, partly by way of oblique excuse for my failure to help her, partly because there wasn't anyone else I could talk about my life with. You see, I'm the eternal bachelor. No woman was ever good enough. (Thank you, Mama!) (Yes, I know, it's an old, old story. Sorry if I bore you!) Anyway, I was telling Anka all this, thinking she might understand, being sort of on the outer edge of my family herself. The more intimate I got, the more intimate I got, if you know what I mean. I told her things I wouldn't tell you, that's for sure. I felt brave complaining about my mother, as if I was tempting fate to blow the lid on me, because (who knows?) Anka might write to her, and then the shit would really hit the fan. Deeper down, of course, I knew very well that Anka was extremely unlikely to write to my mother, so the burden of my rage, my frustration about a life of secrecy and unknowables, was itself a secret between myself and the unknowable Anka. But was she really that unknowable? In my head, as I wrote more and more of the letter, I developed my own picture of her. Traumatized by her father's desertion of her, unhappily married, she was feeling lost in a life without meaning. That's why it had become so important to her to find her roots. She didn't know who she was any more, and was looking to me for help. Maybe we would become friends by correspondence, and as the months, or years, went by, who knows . . . ? Her marriage would probably dissolve, she would be restless, unfocused, confused . . . It was so much easier to get out of Poland these days; the economy was booming, people were allowed to keep their money and travel overseas. All things considered, it was really very likely that I would meet Anka one of these days . . . and she really was very beautiful. Those breasts!

My letter ended up ten pages long. Some of the words in it were a bit technical, but I trusted that Anka could look them up in her dictionary. I was just about to fold the thick wad of paper into an envelope and post it, when the mail arrived and, lo and behold, there was another letter from her.

Dear sir, [it said]

> *Once more I thanks you very much for your effort to help me, it is all right that you are not a success. I have very glad news to passover to you! With international moneyorder I have purchased telephone directorys of your country. This was suggestion of my husband Piotr – he is so clever! We receive these directorys three days ago, and we look at the Ciebulas. There are quite a many, but because Piotr is telecommunicationsengineer he is abled to make some telephones calls at his work and say they are just testing! After merely ten or eleven strange Ciebulas, what do you think happens? I sit abruptly speaking to my father, alive and healthy! He is old man now but his heart is still young. We forgive everything and start again like new, and now he want to come back to Poland to die, but not until Februar. He is very joyous about grandchildren what he did not know he has, and he is sharply wanting photographs. He said that he has no old photographs of him himself, they was all keeped by your mother, but to be downcast is not necessary, because he will go directly to the photoautomat and make new ones, and also soon he will bring us the real man!*
>
> *But there is also space in our life for you! Please, if you are ever travelling in Poland, be invited to visit us.*
>
> *Yours faithfully,*
> *Anka Kwiatkowska*

I folded the letter up (*hers*, that is), and seriously considered throwing it in the bin, to join mine there. After all, this was clearly 'end of story'. However, I put it back into the envelope instead.

What convinced me to keep it, more than anything else,

was the photograph which accompanied her letter. It was a picture of a child, presumably one of Anka's, next to a snowman almost twice his height. He was standing on a stepladder. At least, he *had* been, a split-second before the photograph was taken: the shutter had been pressed just as he'd leaped off the stepladder, his arms thrown wide in joy. The snowman was finished, and in the picture every detail was sharp – turnip-sprouts, bottlecaps, glistens of snow and all. The boy, by contrast, was a colourful blur. Even though I haven't the foggiest idea who he is, I feel such affection for him! It's a great photograph, that's for sure. Along with one of the ones I paid a bloody fortune to get duplicated, it may well become my favourite. And what's the other one? Well, I suppose I can tell you. It's a picture of a whole bunch of Polish guys in overalls sitting in some sort of meeting hall. One of them is my father at about twenty years old, slouched with his arms folded across his chest, as if suffering in silence, the way he always did. But there's about fifty other men there too; fat ones, gawky ones, melancholy looking ones, broad-shouldered hunks, wiry little guys, all sharply alive and keenly attentive. The point is, I like to think that Wojtek Ciebula is in there somewhere, unknown to my father, unknown to my mother. Just *there*, for no other reason than that he was alive then, and living in the same place. It's the sort of possibility my mother would never have thought of, and that's why, going through the photographs years later, scissors in hand, she'd probably have missed him.

HIEROGLYPHICS

Anne Donovan

A mind they were birlin an dancin roon like big black spiders. A couldnae keep a haunle oan them fur every time A thoat A'd captured them, tied them thegither in some kinny oarder they jist kep oan escapin.

Just learn the rules pet. Just learn them off by heart.

But they didnae follow oany rules that A could make sense of. M-A-R-Y. That's ma name. Merry. But that wus spelt different fae merry christmas that you wrote in the cards you made oot a folded up bits a cardboard an yon glittery stuff that comes in thae wee tubes. You pit the glue oan the card an shake the glitter oan it an its supposed tae stick in a nice wee design. It wisnae ma fault, A didnae mean tae drap the whole load ae it oan the flerr. But how come flerr wisnae spelt the same as merry an sterr wis different again an ma heid wis nippin wi coff an laff an though an bow, meanin a bit aff a tree. A thoat it wis Miss Mackay that wis aff her tree, right enough.

A pride of lions
A gaggle of geese
A flock of sheep
A plague of locusts

We hud tae learn aw they collective nouns aff by hert, chantin roon the class every efternoon when we came back in fae wur dinner, sittin wi oor erms foldit lookin oot the

121

high windaes at the grey bloacks a flats an the grey streets, an sometimes the sky wisnae grey but maistly it wis. An A could a tellt you the collective noun for every bliddy animal in the wurld practically, but it wis a bitty a waste when you think oan it. A mean it would a come in handy if Drumchapel ever goat overrun wi lions. You coulda lookt oot the windae at some big hairy oarange beast devourin yer wee sister an turn to yir mammy an say, *Look, Mammy, oor Catherine's been et by a pride of lions*, an huv the comfort a knowin ye were usin the correct terminology, but A huv tae tell you it never happened. No even a floacky sheep ever meandered doon Kinfauns Drive of a Friday evenin (complete wi Mary and her little lamb who had mistaken their way). In fact A never seen any animals barrin Alsation dugs an scabby auld cats till the trip tae the Calderpark Zoo in Primary Four.

She lacks concentration.
She's lazy, ye mean.
No, I don't think she's lazy, there is a genuine difficulty there.
She's eight year auld an she canny read nor write yet.

Ma mammy thoat A wis daft, naw, no daft exactly, no the way wee Helen fae doon the street wis. A mean she didnae even go tae the same school as us an she couldnae talk right an she looked at ye funny an aw the weans tried tae avoid playin wi her in the street. Ma mammy knew A could go the messages an dae stuff roon the hoose an talk tae folk, A wis jist daft at school subjects, the wans that that involved readin or writin oanyway. Fur a while after she went up tae see the teacher A goat some extra lessons aff the Remmy wummin but A hated it. She wis nice tae me at furst but then when A couldnae dae the hings she wis geein me she began tae get a bit scunnered. A hink she thoat A wis lazy, an A could never tell them aboot the letters diddlin aboot, and oanyway, naebdy ever asked me whit it wis like. They gave me aw these tests an heard ma readin an asked me questions, an tellt ma ma A hud a readin age of 6.4 an a spellin age of 5.7 an Goad knows whit else, but naebdy ever asked me whit wis gaun oan in ma heid. So A never tellt them.

An after a while the extra lessons stoaped. They were dead nice tae me at school but. Maisty the time the teacher gied me the colourin in tae dae an when A wis in Primary seven A goat tae run aw the messages an helped oot wi the wee wans. No wi their reading ye understaun, but gettin their paints mixed an takin them tae the toilet an pittin oot the mulk fur them.

Mary is so good with the younger children, I don't know what I'm going to do without my little assistant when she goes to the High School.

A big rid brick buildin bloackin oot the sky. Spiky railins wi green paint peelin aff them. Hard grey tarmac space in front wi weans loupin aw ower the place, playin chasies in the yerd, joukin aboot roon the teachers' motors; the big yins, sophisticated, hingin aboot the coarner, huvin a fly puff afore the bell goes. An us, wee furst years, aw shiny an poalished lookin in wur new uniforms (soon tae be discardit), staunin in front y the main door, waitin tae be tellt where we're gaun.

Just copy the class rules off the board into your jotter.

Anither brand new jotter. Anither set a rules tae coapy. This is the last period a the day an the sixth time A've hud tae dae it. Could they no jist huv wan lot a rules fur every class? It takes me that long tae coapy the rules oot that the lesson's nearly finished an A've missed it. The French teacher took wan look at the dug's dinner A wis producin an tellt me no tae boather, jist tae dae it later.

An the Maths teacher asked me ma name an looked me up in a list.

You're Mary Ryan, are you? Mmm.

Must of been the remmy list. Am no remmy at Maths right enough – it's jist A canny read the stuff. If sumbdy tells me whit tae dae Ah kin usually dae it, A jist canny read it masel in thae wee booklets. It's funny how the numbers never seem tae birl aroon the way the letters dae; mibby its because there urny usually as many numbers in a number as there are letters in a word, if ye kin understaun whit A mean. Or is it because ye read them acroass the way an ye dae maths doon the way? Mibby if A lived in wanny thae countries where they wrote doon the way A'd be aw right. A mean no everybdy writes lik we dae. We dun a project oan it in Primary Five an there's aw kins a ways a writin in the world. Some folk read right tae left an some up an doon. An they Egyptians drew wee pictures fur aw their writin. A hink A should of been an Egyptian.

And what's this supposed to be – hieroglyphics?

A hated that sarky bastard. Mr Kelly. Skelly, we cried him though he wisnae actually skelly; he used tae squint at ye through wan eye as if he wis examinin ye through a microscope an hid jist discovered some new strain a bacteria that could wipe oot the entire population a Glesga. He wis the Latin teacher but he hud hardly oany classes because naebdy done Latin noo so they'd gied him oor class fur English, an then every time a teacher wis aff sick he used tae take the class, so A began seein a loaty him. An that wis bad news.

Ye see A'd never felt lik this afore wi oany ither teachers. A knew whit they were thinkin of me right enough, A could see it in their eyes, but maisty them jist thoat A wis a puir wee sowl that couldnae learn oanythin an so whit wis the point a them tryin ae teach me? Sometimes they even said it oot loud, like when the heidie wis daein his wee dauner roon the classes tae make sure we were aw wurkin hard an no writin graffiti oan oor jotters. (Chance wid a been a fine thing.)

And how are they settling in Miss Niven?

Oh very well, Mr McIver, they're all working very hard on their project on the Egyptians. Amir has produced a wonderful imaginative piece on the last thoughts of Tutankhamen and look how neatly Mary's coloured in the borders of the wall display. [Stage whisper] She's a poor wee soul but she tries very hard.

Obviously no bein able tae read makes ye deif.

But that big skelly bastard wis different. Tae start wi A thoat he wis jist boarin an boredom is sumpn that disnae boather me, Am used tae it, A hink maist weans are. The furst few days he rambled oan aboot grammer an wrote stuff up oan the board an we didnae really hufty dae oanythin bar keep oor mooths shut. Which is easie-peesie tae me. But then he startit tae dictate notes tae us an he could time his pace jist so. If ye kin imagine the class lik a field a racehoarses then he wus gaun at such a pelt that only the first two or three could keep up wi him. The rest wur scribblin furiously, their airms hingin oot thur soackets, sighin an moanin ower their jotters, an then he'd tease them wi a pause that wis jist a toty bit aff bein long enough tae let them catch up, an then, wheech, he wis aff again lik lightnin.

Me, A wis the wan that fell at the furst fence.

A did try but A goat masel intae such a complete fankle that A hud tae stoap writin, an instead a bein lik the ither teachers an jist leavin me in peace or sendin me a message or sumpn he hud tae make hissel smart by drawin attention tae me. Jist a big wean when ye think on it, though it didnae feel that way at the time.

Do you know what hieroglyphics are, Mary?

Aye, sur. It's Egyptian writing.

Yes, sir, not Aye, sir. I is the first person nominative, not that any of you will know what that means, of course, since you no longer have the good fortune to be properly educated in the classical tradition. Maybe if you would learn to speak properly you could then write properly.

The class were aw sittin up lik circus lions at this point, wonderin whit the ringmaister wis gonny dae next. Sometimes he would launch intae a big long speech an then ye didnae huv tae dae oany work. Which wis hunky dory as long as you wereny the wan he'd lamped oanty.

So, Mary, if hieroglyphics means Egyptian writing, why do you think I am referring to your script using that term?

Because you canny . . . can't read it, sir.

Precisely, Mary. And since the function of reading is to communicate, what point is there in writing something which is utterly unintelligible?

A jist sat there.

Well, Mary, I'm awaiting your answer.

But if you were an Egyptian you could read hieroglyphics, sur.

Are you trying to be funny, girl?

No, sur.

I thought not. Well, Mary, since neither you nor I nor anyone in this room appears to hail from ancient Egypt, you are going to have to learn to write in a legible hand. And since you have not managed to write down today's notes then I suggest you borrow someone else's jotter and copy them out tonight.

A wis mortified, pure mortified. The lassie next tae me passed her jotter ower wioot sayin a wurd an A pit it in ma bag an walked oot the room. An from that day sumpn funny startit tae happen that A couldnae unnerstaun. The class stoaped talkin tae me but it wisnae like they'd aw fell oot wi me; A mean if A asked tae borrow their Tippex or said did ye see *Home an Away* last night they wid answer me, but they widnae say much an they never startit a coanversation wi me. An there seemed tae be an empty space aw roon me in the class, fur naebdy sat next tae me if they could help it. A couldny figure it oot, fur they aw hatit auld Skelly, so how come jist because he didny like me they didny either. You'd hink it wid be the ither way roon.

An it wisnae jist in his class either, A couldy unnerstood that aw right fur who wants tae sit near the target practice? But it wis in every ither class tae, an the playgrun an the dinner school. An when ye move up tae the big school it's a time when friendships kinny shuffle roon lik wanny they progressive barn dances, an ye make new wans an ye lose auld wans an somehow in the middly aw this process A fun masel oot the dance wioot a partner. An it wisnae nice.

Then A startit daein the hieroglyphics fur real. In the beginnin it wis party oor History project oan the Egyptians. We aw hud tae make up oor ain version, writin wee messages an stories. Miss Niven presented it tae us as if it wis some crackin new original idea though of course we done it in Primary Four (but we didnae tell her that cos it wis better n readin aboot the preservation a mummies). An A turnt oot tae be dead good at it. Somehow the wee pictures jist seemed tae come intae ma heid an it wis that easy compared tae writin wurds. If ye wanted tae say would you like a cup of tea? ye jist drew a wee cupnsaucer an a mooth wi an arra pointin at it an pit a question mark. Nae worryin aboot whit kinny wood it wis or how many Es in tea.

An gradually A progressed fae writin wee messages tae writin whole stories in wee pictures. A spent ages gettin them jist right an colourin them in wi felties an Miss Niven even gied me a special fine black pen fur daein the outlines. An the rest a the class moved oantae the Second World War but A stayed in ancient Egypt, stuck in a coarner a the room wi a pile a libry books roon me, drawin they wee sideyways people wi their big fish eyes. They used tae get buried wi aw the hings they thoat they'd need in their next life, they even took their pieces wi them, an it set me wonderin, whit would A huv took wi me intae ma next life, but then how would ye know whit it wis gonny be like? It's a bit lik gaun tae Err fur the day – will ye be runnin aboot oan the beach in yer shorts or sittin in the café wi five jumpers oan, watchin the rain pour doon? An if ye canny prepare yersel fur a day at the seaside how the hell ur ye gonny dae it fur yer next life?

An the mair A studied they libry books the mair A could see things huvny changed aw that much since the time a the Egyptians. They hud goads that were hauf-human an hauf-animal an as A looked at their pictures A saw the faces a ma teachers. So A drew some gods ae ma ain. Miss Niven wus a wee tweetery wumman, aye dartin roon the classroom so A gied her the boady ae a wumman an the heid ae a wee speug, coacked tae wan side. Then their wis Mr Alexander, hauf-man, hauf-fish cos he wis aye losin the place. Auld Kelly hud grey crinkly herr like a judge's wig an a big baw face so he hud tae be a ram wi huge curly hoarns, jist like the Egyptian god ae the underworld. Very appropriate, that. An Ah wis jist tryin tae work oot whether the heidie wis mair lik the Sun god or a sphinx, when he swpt intae the room.

Miss Niven, the Quality Assurance Unit will be visiting the school next Tuesday, nothing to worry about, just an informal visit to pick out good practice.

Will they want to see my planning sheets?

Yes, but I'm sure all your paperwork is up to date, and there is evidently splendid work going on the room. But what is this child doing drawing pictures of Egyptians? Should she not be on to the 'Victory for Democracy' Unit by now?

So the next day ma felties an cardboard were pit away an A hud tae dae a worksheet oan the Russian front. She let me keep the wee fine black pen though, she's dead nice, Miss Niven.

But Skelly Kelly wis still a bastard an A goat him every day a the week. An his teachin wisnae even as modern as the ancient Egyptians, oot the ark, mair like; aw ye did wis write write, write till yer erm felt lik a big balloon or ye hud tae dae grammar exercises an interpretations, an he never read us stories lik the ither English teachers. An because A couldnae dae aw the writin in time A ended up takin piles a stuff hame tae coapy up every night, then he took the jotters in wanst a week an mines came back covered in red marks. Ma writin looked a bit lik wee scarab beetles scurryin aboot the page an when he corrected it, it wis as if the wee beetles hud aw startit bleedin.

Once again, Mary Ryan, I can barely read a word of your writing.

A couldnae unnerstaun a word of whit he wrote oan ma jotter either but A couldnae very well say that, could A?

An then wan day A couldnae take it oany longer.

Today you will be doing a timed composition. This is to give you practice for your examinations. The question is on the board. You have precisely fifty minutes. Begin.

Imagine you are going on a journey. Describe where you are going and what things you would take with you.

So A startit tae write aboot ma journey tae the next wurld an the hings A wid take wi me, aw in wee pictures. A drew me n ma mammy (ma da might as well be in the next wurld fur aw A see of him) an ma sisters, Catherine an Elizabeth in a wee boat, fur A hud some idea that A wanted ma journey tae be ower the watter. An we took nice stuff tae eat, big plates a mince an tatties (A know ye couldnae really keep them hoat but it kinna makes sense the way the Egyptians dae it) an ice cream fae the café an boals a ginger n sweeties n at.

A spent a loang time thinkin oot whit else A wanted tae take, fur a loaty the hings we huv in this wurld might no be oany use tae us in the next. After aw, whit use are Take That records if there wis nae electricity? So A decided tae gie each ae us three hings tae take in the boat fur ye widnae want that much stuff that the boat wid sink, an oanyway three is wanny they numbers that's gey important in stories. Who ever heardy emdy gettin five wishes aff their fairy goadmother or two blin mice or the seventeen wee pigs?

Elizabeth's three hings were easy fur she's only four an she aye kerries a bitty auld blanket roon wi her, an she won't go oanywhere wioot her teddy or her Sindy doll. Catherine's eight but she would need tae take her teddy too an her new blue jumper wi a picture y a wee lamb oan it an her deelie-boablers, ye know they hings ye pit roon yer heid lik an alice band but they've goat wee antennaes stickin oot fae them an they make ye look lik sumpn fae ooter space. A know these kinny hings go in an ooty fashion an two weeks fae noo she'll feel lik a real chookie when she minds she wanted tae go tae mass in them, but at the moment she'd want tae take them. An A'd take some paper an the black pen fur daein ma hiero-glyphics an ma picture ae a wee spaniel pup that A cut ooty a magazine an keep oan the wall by ma bed, fur we couldnae huv a real dug doon ma bit.

But whit would ma mammy take wi her? Aw ae a sudden

it came tae me that A didnae know whit ma mammy wid take oan her journey tae the next wurld, it wid need tae be sumpn private an jist fur her, an mammys don't tell ye these things fur they're too busy wurkin an bringin ye up tae huv a loaty time fur theirsels. An then auld Kelly told us tae finish oaff, it wis time, so A hud tae leave her wi naethin. But mibby no, fur A hink if A'd asked her, ma mammy wid say we are her three best hings, Catherine an Elizabeth n me.

Mary Ryan will collect in the compositions.

A walked roon the class, gaitherin in the bits a paper, lookin at each wan as A picked it up. Aw they different kinds of haunwritin; squinty, straight, big or wee, aw different sizes an shapes oan the page. Then A picked up ma ain story wi its neat wee black drawins an noticed A hudny pit ma name oan it. So A drew a wee picture a masel wi a cheery face oan it, pit ma story right oan tap ae the pile an planted the whole lot doon in the centre a his desk.

MY SON, MY SON

John Spence

Not in the least. No, not at all. Any chance I get, I like to
tell people what really happened. Not so much for myself,
you understand, but for the boy; he can't speak for himself, not any more.

So, how do you want to do this? Question and answer,
or me telling the story and you interrupting if I go too
fast or miss things out? What I *don't* want, mind you, is
having my name tacked on to a lot of stuff you've made
up. There's been too much of that.

To understand what happened, and why, you have to
go back to when the boy and I first arrived in Crete, or
soon after. I'd run into a bit of trouble in Athens and
thought it was time for a change. So we crossed the sea
to Knossos, set up a workshop, took on a few jobs, built up
quite a nice little business. They liked the fiddly, arty-crafty
stuff, not really to my taste, but the money was good. Then
King Minos sent for me.

Royal families! Oh boy! They thought they were like
the gods, you see, and could do anything they wanted.
Pasiphae, the queen. Extraordinary woman. Part Egyptian,
I think. Absolutely, oh, indescribable. So beautiful you
were almost afraid to touch her. Almost. But problems,
oh, by Aphrodite, what problems! Couldn't get enough,
you see. Don't need to spell it out, men of the world.
Anyone, eventually, and maybe anything.

You'll have heard the stories about her and the

bull. I don't know. Not true about me being taken on to make the – the structure, the sham cow. That had happened – if it happened – before the boy and I arrived. Easy enough, I suppose, but can't have been very comfortable, and, well, the practicalities. Just think about it. There would have been damage, must have been. And there wasn't. Well, how do you think I'd know? Bloody fool. OK, OK.

No, what Minos wanted me to do was plan and build a cellar conversion, what we call a labyrinth, where they could keep the poor little sod, Pasiphae's boy. Oh, terrible, you can't imagine. His head all deformed, funny shape and, yes, what looked like horns. Might have done better if they hadn't hidden him away, never saw daylight, looked after by dumb slaves. Because their tongues were cut out. Well, they were only slaves. Yes, yes, all right.

You may have something, though. Not a nice place, Knossos, behind all the pretty painted walls. There's hurting people, and usually feeling sorry afterwards, because you're in a hurry, or want something very badly and they get in the way. And there's hurting people because you enjoy it. Minos was the second kind. If you were in favour it was a wonderful place, beautiful women, very liberated, ah, yes. But if you upset him, very nasty indeed, quite ingeniously nasty.

Anyway, working in and under the palace I saw a lot of Pasiphae, got to know her quite well. Usual thing, came down to see how the work was going, oh, are you in charge, and did you draw up the plans and everything, how clever, and the look – weighing you up – there may be someone interesting here, and the little glance sideways on – *you* know – and the wiggle and the silk skirt rustling over the hips. Aah!

Never, never, anyone like her. Happens so often, they hook you, reel you in and throw you back, 'I can't imagine how you ever thought . . .' Load of bullshit. But Pasiphae followed through, oh yes.

And nothing and no one to get in the way. Minos didn't care. Some kind of problem. Well, must have been. It looked as though he was glad to have her entertained by someone else, so long as it wasn't too public. And that caused a bit of difficulty.

Exactly. Like a *gynaeceum* in reverse, locked in the labyrinth. She didn't like her lovers to waste energy on other things, I suppose – or meet other women. *Her* story was, Minos would get upset if he thought I was able to stroll around Knossos boasting about how well I knew the queen. So for my own protection it was better I should stay in the labyrinth. She said the guards were just for the look of the thing, though they didn't seem to think so. Hard luck on the boy, though, Icarus, because he was locked up with me.

But on balance it was very, *very* nice, even after I discovered how possessive she was and she began to make me play along with her fantasy about the bull. Maybe how the story about Poseidon's bull started. So when she wanted, which was quite often, I had to get togged up in a bull-hide, wear an imitation bull's head, even make bull noises. You probably think I was silly. No? I'm glad. She's the only woman I've ever known who could have made me do anything like that – and it wasn't because she was the queen. You understand? Yes, once in a lifetime, and you're liable to finish up broke, ruined, no friends left and still think it was worth it.

Even the dressing up as a bull, knowing I was only an actor in her fantasy, that it wasn't really me. Ever felt like that, known a woman was thinking about someone else? And how did you feel? Ha! That he was only getting fond thoughts while you were enjoying the kisses and cuddles! Yes, I like that. I like a man with a sense of humour.

Usually goes with a generous nature. Ah, thank you. Not much left, is there? Why not open another bottle now, let it breathe?

Sometimes felt a bit closed in – more sorry for Icarus, really, but he got quite fond of the bull-boy. Taught him a few words. Couldn't get him trained, though. Oh, everywhere. Talk about the Augean stables! Phew! Tested the ventilation, I can tell you, however hard the slaves worked to keep the place clean. We could live with it, though, and things weren't too bad until Minos decided to join the game.

On what turned out to be the last night I was wearing my bull outfit and as usual after we finished Pasiphae lay propped up on the pillows and I had to lie with my head – inside the bull's head – in her lap and pretend to go to sleep. I lay there while she stroked the bull's head and talked to it in her usual way. But this night, the one I'm talking about, it was me, the real me, she was talking to, only she thought I was asleep and couldn't hear what she said.

'Deedles –' that was what she used to call me – 'it's been lovely. I don't think anyone's ever given me so much fun, but it's time for you to go down below,' and she kept stroking the head – I could feel the vibration – and murmuring.

I had to stay in character as the wild bull she had satisfied and tamed, but pretending to be asleep became more and more difficult. She kept talking softly, as though to herself, how she didn't want to let me go, but Minos wouldn't allow her to keep one man for too long. In case she got too fond of him, I suppose, or he got ambitious.

'This is your last night with me, last night with any woman. Poor Deedles, what a waste! Tomorrow at noon they'll come for you, then you'll be Minos's toy instead of mine. Maybe I'll see you in the court – he keeps my old lovers alive and brings them out to play with sometimes, but you won't see me, of course. Or anything.'

You can imagine how it felt, lying there, listening to her sweet voice murmur those dreadful things, not able to escape. No, I couldn't get out of the head or the bull-hide without her help. Straps and fastenings I couldn't reach. If what she said was true I had a few hours to play with – she usually sent me back down to the labyrinth before dawn – but everything depended on Minos's plan. A door in her room opened on a stairway leading down into the labyrinth, with doors at the top and the bottom. In the early days she used to call a guard to take me downstairs and bolt the lower door behind me. Later, when she trusted me more, I suppose, she left me to go down on my own, though she still bolted the upper door. *If* Minos and his men weren't coming for me until noon I had a chance. What I was afraid of, though, was opening the door and finding a guard on the staircase, or Pasiphae calling one, probably more than one, to bind me and keep me quiet until Minos arrived.

I was worried about the boy, too. He was sixteen, a big, strapping lad and I had seen Pasiphae cast an eye over him when she came down to visit the bull-boy. Maybe he was next in line and I didn't think he was ready. A woman like Pasiphae, well, she'd be too much for a youngster to cope with. Oh, he'd learn a lot very quickly, but he wouldn't know how to pace himself, for example. And when she got tired of him . . .

After what seemed like years she woke me, as she thought, took the bull's head off and started kissing me. Then she pulled back, helped me out of the hide, said goodbye 'until tomorrow night' and pushed me through the door opening on to the staircase. I heard her bolt it behind me.

I still don't know how I got down those stairs. Naked,

unarmed, shitting myself with terror. Any moment I expected hands to seize me, to feel the ropes and cudgels. And later, not only the cutting and gouging, but the fetters. May the gods forgive me, I've been part of the system myself, in Athens. I've seen how a man looks when the cuffs on his neck and wrists and ankles are hammered shut and he realizes what the rest of his life is going to be like.

So, more frightened with every step, I got to the door at the bottom. I thought they might be waiting for me there, but there was nothing I could do but go on. I opened the door very slowly and crept through as quietly as I could, pausing between each step to listen for the sound of breathing or the clink of a weapon. Not a sound.

Then, the next problem. They might be waiting for me further on. I could pick one of three ways to get back to our quarters. Which to choose? The obvious place for them to lie in wait for me was on the shortest way, so I would take one of the others. But wouldn't they expect me to do just that? Minos was the only other person with a plan of the labyrinth and he might have worked out what I was most likely to do. Devious bastard. Even more devious than me. Bluff, double bluff, triple bluff, get so clever you fall over your own feet. I must have stood there for ages, trying to work it out, trying to decide. You know how it is when you're really frightened? You can imagine? No, I don't think you can.

What? Oh, I didn't believe I was safe until noon. That's an old trick; they give you time to dig up the money you've hidden, lead them to your friends. No. A bit of advice. As soon as you get the word, run. Forget about going home to collect your treasures and arrange for someone to feed the cat. Just go, if you want to stay free and whole.

At last I made up my mind, chose the shortest way, woke the boy by putting my hand over his mouth and told him in a whisper to get dressed. No questions, no argument, do it. When we both had our clothes on I picked up my tools and money and we got ready to leave.

More advice. If a king, or any powerful man, asks you to design and build a labyrinth where he can keep something or someone hidden, and especially if he lets you see who or what he's hiding, build yourself an exit, one nobody else knows about. The way I work, doing a lot of it myself because I've no patience with learners, except Icarus and not even him sometimes, it was easy. After everyone else knocked off I'd stay on, say I wanted to get things set up so the unskilled people had something they could start on straight away next morning. Nothing worse than hands hanging around. Bad planning. So we had our escape hatch, if someone hadn't built a house on top of it. And they hadn't.

Icarus was a bit unhappy about leaving the bull-boy without saying goodbye, but when he smelled the fresh air and saw the stars he got too excited to think about anything else. Oh, six months or thereabouts. Yes, a long time.

We lay low until it was properly daylight and people were moving about, then headed for the hills. I knew Minos would have men searching for us as soon as he knew we were gone and the first place they'd look would be the seaports and the coast in general. So I thought the hills would be safer. When the hunt died down we might be able to get a passage on a ship. But it didn't die down.

For a few months we moved from village to village. Anyone who can repair ploughs and sickles will always get by. I suppose it's my sort of basic trade, smithing and metalwork, though I can turn my hand to anything. But the boy wasn't learning anything worthwhile and you get tired of being hunted. Then one day I noticed the birds. Exactly. How the big raptors can hover without flapping their wings, riding the air currents. And I noticed how on a hot day the air above shiny, reflective ground rises. Yes, thermals. Fancy you knowing about them and the name I gave them!

This is the part of the story everybody knows, or thinks they know, except they get the important bits wrong. Like Pasiphae helping us escape from the labyrinth. Pathetic. And the wings. Flapping wings! Just think. We're the wrong shape, our muscles are in the wrong places and we haven't got the power. Back to the thermals. Let the air do the work. Man provides the skill and intelligence. And courage.

Which was the problem. You have to get it right first time; no chance to practise. But we worked it out. Rigid wings fixed to a central framework and movable flaps controlled by levers to let you go up and down and turn. We made the frames of wooden spars, covered the wings with strips of oiled cloth stuck down and varnished, and made body harnesses of leather straps. I picked the ideal place, a high steep cliff above a long stretch of scree, where we could launch ourselves and pick up a thermal. By midmorning there's usually a breeze off the sea, which I thought would help. Quite simple. Face the right way, take a run at it and jump. Simple. But not easy.

We'd probably have been there now, checking and rechecking, taking it in turns to tow each other on a line, get the feel of the controls, putting off the moment we would have to jump, but Minos made up our mind for us. He found out where we were and came after us with his soldiers. Not just a patrol; more like a company. Oh, somebody's husband, maybe. I know, but you can't be sensible all the time, not if you've got anything about you. That was all we needed, really, just the thought of being taken back to Knossos, and the little sharp knives and the fettered darkness.

139

I'd made a sort of path for us, carried away loose stones, filled up holes, so we could have a clear run off the edge of the cliff. Not a good time to trip or stumble. I went first.

Took a lot of doing, I can tell you, keeping up the pace for that last couple of yards to the edge and taking the leap into space, seeing the rocks far below. For a moment I thought it wasn't going to work, then I felt the air hold me up. I'll never forget the feeling – terror, then gladness and the satisfaction of knowing we'd worked it all out properly. Icarus followed straight after me, good lad. As we wheeled over the scree, gaining enough height for the next stage, we called to each other, 'We've done it, we're flying!'

I planned to hop from island to island, gaining enough height over each one to glide to the next, but just enough with a little to spare. We didn't really know what it was like up there, whether there was some kind of ceiling, or Zeus might get annoyed because we were trespassing. So I told the boy, stay behind me, don't climb too high.

The silly thing is, we had passed the worst bit, from Cape Sidero to Scarpanto and the tiny islands in the southern part of the Dodecanese. I was looking forward to reaching the mainland and being able to land, have a drink. Funny, you don't think about things like carrying water. Although the weight might have been a problem.

Over Naxos there was a wonderful, strong thermal, took us up in no time. When I thought I had gained enough height I left the thermal, heading north for Hermopolis. Next thing, I heard a shout, sort of jeering, 'You've lost it!'

I banked and looked round. He was swooping and swirling above me, still in the thermal, getting far too high. *'Fool!'* I shouted. 'Come down!'

I don't think the sun melted the gum – in fact, it gets

cooler as you climb. Like mountains. Maybe he thought he was a bird, swooping about like that. You know what happened. All it took was one panel working loose, I suppose, extra strain on the others, lost them all. I saw him fall, trailing strips of cloth – possibly how people got the idea of feathers – and heard the long cry fading down into the sea. My son, my son.

The worst thing – well, one of the worst things – the last words he heard from me were in anger. Oh, I know, I know, everyone feels guilty. I know you mean well, but don't distract me. Something I have to face, reason I've drunk so much wine, painful.

He was a good boy, never complained, even in the labyrinth, worked hard, would have done well. But I never told him I was pleased with him, always told him he could have done better. Only wanted to keep him up to the mark. The trouble is, I don't know if he realized I loved him. I have a feeling he thought I was disappointed in him. And my last words as he fell out of the sky, angry, calling him a fool.

And this is what I want you to say, that he *was* a good boy, not a fool, not showing off. If you can tell them that, so everyone knows, I'll – I'll be obliged.

PICTURES OF IVY

Leslie Hills

Ivy is drying the few dishes she has used for her solitary lunch. One plate, one cup, one saucer, one knife, fork and a teaspoon. She is a small woman in her late seventies moving with precise and practised economy in the tiny kitchen where everything has its place and stays in it. She returns the final piece of cutlery to the drawer, wipes the sink and hangs the teatowel on its appointed hook, to dry. She picks up a paper bag, smooths and folds it carefully and places it in the drawer reserved for useful paper bags. She looks around. Formica and stainless steel gleam. Everything is satisfactory.

A mirror. In the mirror, a face. Ivy is preparing to go out. She dons a hat to match her nondescript, neat, belted, beige raincoat. She applies lipstick firmly and blots it. She checks her image for signs of immodesty or difference and finds none. She turns on small Hush Puppy feet to survey her sitting room. The furniture is neatly ordered as it should be in a mature council semi, purchased ten years since but lived in by Ivy for the past fifty years. Her pink lady's armchair and the gentleman's armchair, empty these five years, flank a small sofa. She moves to the mantelpiece and looks along the photographs arranged there. Grim images of her defunct husband, aged twenty to seventy, posed holding their baby son; with his rink after winning the bowling club cup; with his fellow elders in front of a small brick-built kirk; almost smiling, stiff with pride beside their grown son in rented graduation gown ... posed, sepia through black-and-white box Brownie to fully automatic colour ... There is one small picture of Ivy in wartime wedding suit, looking too young.

Ivy stands on her doorstep inspecting the day. She carries an old-fashioned shopping bag. She double locks the door, takes a tissue from her pocket and rubs at a tiny blemish on the letterbox. As she turns, a neighbour woman passes the gate. They smile distantly. Ivy walks down her short garden path, bending to discipline a weed, opens and closes her gate and walks down the deserted, neat suburban crescent.

Ivy is returning her book to the library. It appears deserted. She walks to the shelves. She finds the section marked romance. Her hand rises, hovers and falls. She stands staring at an island display. One particularly daft cover for a romantic novel catches her eye. A tiny chuckle escapes and is quickly covered by a small cough. In the after-silence there is the sound of childish laughter. Ivy follows the sound. As she rounds the end of a stack she comes upon a group of a dozen infants sitting on a carpet. A librarian reads to them. They are absorbed. Ivy watches. The librarian turns the book to show the children a picture and in doing so catches sight of Ivy. The children turn to stare. Ivy offers a stiff, apologetic smile and disappears behind a pillar.

In a quiet mini-market Ivy is browsing. In her basket are a small piece of cheese, a small packet of flour and a small box of macaroni. She reaches for a pint of milk. The assistant wordlessly punches the till. Ivy pays and accepts her change.

In a small pre-modern café Ivy sits alone. The other occupants are an elderly couple dressed in the beige uniform. They ignore each other, and Ivy. Ivy drinks carefully in the dim silence but as she replaces her cup her teaspoon rattles. Ivy smiles apologetically.

Ivy is leaving the café. She shuts the door carefully. She passes assorted shops and stops to cross the road. Behind her on the corner is a pub. As she waits at the kerb the pub door opens and a man holds it wide while he calls his thanks to the barman. Laughter, music and chatter spill into the street. Ivy stares as the door swings to.

The suburban crescent, as usual, is deserted. Ivy comes into view. She is nearly home. She walks firmly and with purpose. Suddenly she slows, her face loses its composure. She stands stock-still. She drops her shopping bag. Ivy sits down on someone else's wall. She takes off her hat. Her sparse hair blows in the wind.

A dozen patients, among them several elderly, sit in two rows on either side of a hospital corridor, Ivy in the middle of one row. There is the usual studied air of minding-your-own-business and the abandonment of hope. Ivy alone is looking around with a pleasant, vaguely expectant air. She does not wear a hat and her lipstick has wandered a bit. She makes up her mind and starts to sing. Her voice is old and true. She sings 'I'm ower young tae marry yet'. By the time she reaches ' 'Tw'ad be a sin, tae tak me frae ma mammy, yet', the air is thick with embarrassment but no one intervenes.

Receptionists behind a desk at the end of the corridor confer dubiously. When she finishes, two old gents clap, slowly. She acknowledges this graciously and launches into 'O wert thou in the cauld blast'. This is too much for the receptionists. One approaches. 'Come on now, gran, that's enough.' Ivy does not miss a beat. 'Come on now . . .' She takes Ivy's arm. One of the old gents gets up and crosses the corridor. Ivy sings on. The old gent clears his throat and speaks. 'Get your hands off her.' The receptionist is embarrassed. 'I just want her to stop singing.' She takes Ivy by the shoulders. 'Come on now . . .' Ivy has reached 'I'd shelter thee, I'd shelter thee.' The old gent is becoming heated. 'Leave her alone!' The second old gent gets up and crosses to them. He shakes his head, placating. 'This is silly. Please.' Ivy sings on. The receptionist is trying to coax her to her feet. The old gent tries to stop her. The second old gent tries to stop him. Another receptionist pushes the panic button and male nurses appear from everywhere. The second old gent hits the floor. Everyone takes sides. There is utter chaos in the corridor.

A young woman doctor approaches Ivy's door. She stops to look in the sitting-room window. Ivy is in her pink chair slightly off-centre and facing the window. She is talking animatedly. There is no one else in the room. When she sees the doctor she smiles, beautifully.

Ivy and the doctor are in the kitchen. It is littered with dirty dishes and frozen food packets. Ivy is rummaging under some debris and emerges triumphant with the teapot. She sloshes the contents in the sink, takes a teabag from a gaping packet and pours in hot water from the kettle. As she does so the doctor judges it a good time to say, 'Ivy, I think we'd better get you a home help . . .' Ivy is astonished. 'Nonsense. I can manage fine. I've discovered these.' She holds aloft a frozen food package. 'You put it in the oven and eat it. You don't even need a plate! . . .

All these years . . .' She picks up the teapot and spills some tea. She looks at it. 'Shit!' she says happily. The doctor reacts.

The doctor and Ivy are drinking tea in her sitting room. Displaced objects peer from under cushions and all the photos are face down on the mantelpiece. There are several large plates of biscuits and assorted cups laid out on a low table on which there is also a small automatic camera. The doctor puts down her cup. 'We have the results of your tests, Ivy.' Ivy is distracted, looking out the window. 'Oh, yes . . .' The doctor tries to gain her attention. 'We think you suffered a number of cerebral infarctions . . . little tiny strokes . . .' Ivy squares up. 'Tell me, doctor, is that why I feel so good?' 'Good?' says the doctor. 'Alive. I could do anything. If it wasn't for this bag of old bones.' The doctor smiles, 'The condition sometimes does seem to shift a few inhibitions.' Ivy smiles wistfully back, 'About time too . . . I suppose you've been in a pub, doctor?' The doctor admits she has been known . . . Ivy is far away, imagining it. The doctor breaks in, 'The wee strokes might mean that you're not quite so good at things as you used to be.' Ivy reaches behind her, searches under a cushion and produces with a flourish some terminally tangled knitting. The doctor looks concerned and sympathetic. Ivy stares at it and begins to chuckle merrily. The doctor joins in. The offending knitting is cast in the wastepaper bin. The doctor becomes serious. She has remembered something, 'Do you do anything that might be . . . dangerous. You don't drive, do you?' Ivy shakes her head, 'No, no. I did learn, but I never sat a test. It was too . . . complicated. Lewis loved his car.' The two women stare at each other. Bleak. The doctor breaks the mood by indicating the massed cups and biscuits. 'Are you expecting visitors?' Ivy becomes brisk. 'I'm considering redecoration.' She holds out the local newspaper. 'Lewis always did it himself . . .' She shudders . . . 'but it's easy. You choose a firm and ring them up and they come to estimate . . .' She shows the doctor the column of painters and decorators. Ten are marked with large blue crosses. She drops the paper and proffers the automatic camera. 'Will you take my photo? I always took the photos.' The doorbell rings. Ivy ignores it until the picture is taken.

Ivy is in her lobby at the open door. A painter is standing expectantly on the doorstep, clutching a notebook, pencil and measuring tape. Ivy is gracious, 'How good of you to come, Mr Brown. Come away in.' The painter enters and Ivy closes the door.

In the sitting room the painter sits in the gentleman's armchair drinking tea. Two others are taking measurements. The little room seems very full. Ivy is crossing out the third name. She looks up brightly at the doctor, 'I thought a nice stripe.' The doorbell rings.

It is night. Ivy's lobby is dim. Light spills from the sitting room. An ancient leather trunk is being propelled inch by inch towards the sitting-room door. Ivy is sitting on the floor with her back against the trunk, shoving it towards her goal. She is humming 'Bonnie Wee Thing'.

Ivy's face appears in the sitting-room mirror. She is perkily adjusting a hat. It is a large black straw with a dead yellow bird affixed to the brim. She smiles and steps back. She is wearing a smart waisted coat of forties vintage. She picks up a black patent handbag, checks that her purse is in it, puts on high-heeled slippers and leaves the room. Over floor and furniture is scattered the remains of her salad days, half in, half out of open suitcases and plastic bags and the trunk – rayon and crepe dresses, Hebe sports costumes, a feather boa, assorted silly hats ... On the mantelpiece are a collection of very recent photographs of Ivy at various places around Edinburgh. In some she poses, dressed to kill, with denizens of the streets – tramps and beggars and policemen – smiling for Ivy. In pride of place is one of Ivy with ten painters, taken by the doctor.

Ivy is alighting from a bus far out beyond the suburbs on the Forth estuary. She strolls along the drive by the shore. There is a wide sweeping view across the estuary to Fife. The river is calm. The sky is immense. She walks, solitary, in an empty landscape. She stops and looks over the wall down to the sea. The yellow bird, tethered to her hat, bobs in the breeze. Ivy is remembering something wonderful that happened here. She puts down her bag, and runs her hands down her cheeks and cups her chin. She purses her lips and presses them, eyes closed, to the back of her hand. Her arms cross her breasts and encircle her. She is caressing her back like a lover. She sways slightly. She is chuckling. She roars with laughter.

Ivy is trudging the long road to Granton. The scenery is breathtaking but Ivy is tired. In the distance she can see buildings, towers, cranes, but they are a long way off. Ivy's feet are hurting. A car approaches. Standing by the road, Ivy thumbs a lift. The car does not stop. And another ... No luck. Ivy trudges along, head down, thumbing automatically.

A car draws up behind her. She turns with a beatific smile, hat crooked, nylons laddered. It is a police car. Ivy recommences walking. A constable approaches. 'Can we help you?' Ivy does not look at him. 'No, thank you. I'm out for a walk.' The constable looks doubtful and then amused. 'I think you'd better come with us.' Ivy walks doggedly on. 'No, thank you.' From behind he takes her arm. 'Come on now...' Ivy turns round and wildly knees him in the groin. He falls to the ground. In the follow-through of her swing, Ivy falls on top of him. Groans and chuckles mingle.

It is late. The doctor is in her office. She is talking on the telephone. 'I think you had better come. Well, I first noticed she was talking to herself and there have been little ... the police really would like to ... there was an incident ... no ... no one ... she attacked a policeman. ... Yes ... your mother ... I think you'd better ... Tomorrow then.' The doctor replaces the phone.

In Ivy's sitting room the suitcases have been tidied away. Her son, a quiet man in his fifties in a suit, is looking with concern and love at his mother, seated in her pink chair. Her garb today is this side of eccentric. The doctor makes up the triangle. Ivy is expostulating, 'I never talked to myself in my whole life ... I should have! There wasn't much conversation between these four walls. It's a wonder I didn't talk to myself. But if I didn't then, I'm certainly not starting now. At my age!' The doctor is gentle. 'Tell us about the singing, Ivy. In the hospital.' Ivy brightens. 'Everybody looked so sad. I was sitting there. They were sitting there. I was so bored. The place was like a tomb. Everybody needed cheering up.' She stops. The doctor looks at the son; leans forward, 'Yes?' Ivy explains the obvious, 'So I sang them a song. They were bored. I sang them a song. I don't know what all the fuss was about ... Is he all right?' She turns to the doctor. 'He'll be OK. Broken bones do take a while to mend at his age.' Ivy's son speaks gently, 'And the policeman, Ma?' Ivy is concerned. 'What do you mean? ... Surely I didn't actually break anything? . . . I thought . . .' Her son smothers a smile. 'You didn't break anything, Ma. But what happened?' Ivy sighs. 'I went to the river to walk back to Granton. It's been years. I've always loved that place. I went there with my dad and later with others . . . and we'd walk home along the shore.' She brightens. 'I got up to a few things on that beach, I can tell you.' She is miles away. Her son brings her back: '. . . The policeman?' Ivy shrugs. 'I got tired and I tried to hitch a lift. I've seen them do it. It's not against the law, is it? Then he tried to make me come with him . . . and I saw red. I never knew what that meant before. They shouldn't grab you like that . . . not even policemen. I'd read about what to do. I'd always wondered if I'd get it right. I hit the button, though, didn't I?' She smiles guiltily, gleefully at her son. 'You did that, Ma . . . And what are you going to do next? I have to go back to London soon and I won't be easy leaving you.' He turns to the doctor. 'Can I leave Ma? She seems well, and . . . happy. She wants to stay here, don't you, Ma, and she has enough money to be independent, if she's careful.' The doctor looks at him. Time passes. She turns to Ivy. 'Are you lonely?' Ivy is amazed. 'Not at all! I have plenty of people to talk to. You have no idea. There are so many young people sitting in the streets these days. We talk. Sometimes we have a cup of tea. And then of course I have my voices.' Ivy beams into the silence which is broken by her son who speaks carefully, 'Your voices?' Ivy turns and reaches for her telephone. 'Watch,' she says. 'This was about the best thing you ever got me. And I was annoyed because it was for OAPs!' She smiles at her son fondly. The telephone has large buttons and a speaker button. She presses the speaker button which glows red and then dials an 0898 number. A chatline jingles. A telephone rings. She settles back. A voice from the speaker fills the room, 'Hello? This is Darren.' Ivy is apologetic but brisk. 'Hello, Darren. I'm Ivy. I'm afraid I haven't time for a chat just now but perhaps we'll have a talk later. Bye-bye.' She hangs up. 'See? It's legal. I've my own code.' She chuckles. 'But I'm glad there are no pictures. You can get away with a lot on the telephone . . .'

Son and mother are on Granton pier in his parked car. It is old, small, nondescript. The pier juts out into the wide river. They are quite isolated. She is pointing at a row of two-up two-down houses across the bay. 'Seven children. How she managed, I'll never know . . . the only money I ever had to myself was the dead money.' Her son is not looking at the little house. He is looking at his mother. 'Dead money?' Ivy takes a moment to answer, 'Yes. We used to look regularly. Once, I must have been about ten. It was a winter's night and dark. I was lucky. I found this man. You had to be quick in case someone came along . . . before you'd got the money. Funny, they always had money. This time there was a ten-shilling note. Riches beyond belief. Why would someone jump in the river with ten shillings in his pocket?' Ivy's son is learning a lot about this woman who has been his mother for fifty years. 'How did you know where . . . ?' Ivy is far in the past. 'It's something to do with the currents. We always knew where to look. I dried out the ten-shilling note on the range. I gave it to my ma. It was too much to keep . . . Often she had no money . . .'

Ivy and her son are in a solicitor's office, seated in front of his desk. Ivy is smartly dressed, forties style, and wears gloves in honour of the occasion. The solicitor is business-like. 'Now, Mrs Primrose – your full name is Ivy Primrose?' Ivy grins, 'I should never have married him.' The solicitor takes this to mean yes. 'You are aware that by giving your son power of attorney you are empowering him to act for you in all things?' Ivy looks him square in the eye, 'Of course. I'm a lot dafter than I look, you know.'

Ivy is at her sitting-room window waving to her son who is driving off. She sits down, punches the telephone and settles down for a chat with Kylie, or Tracey or Terry . . .

It is night. Ivy is dressed in her best. She walks towards the pub. Then past it. She returns and enters the pub, in a rush. It is a local with a friendly genial atmosphere. There are a number of groups at tables. One table where four young people are deep in conversation has a vacant seat. Ivy sits down and waits. A barman is setting up a microphone. Ivy watches as people go to the bar. She understands. She rises and goes to the bar. As she does so, the barman is heard in the background introducing the bar quiz night. Ivy is oblivious. She is concentrating. The barmaid approaches. 'Yes, dear?' Ivy whispers, 'A medium-dry sherry, please,' and is relieved when the barmaid smiles and complies. As she waits for and pays for her drink she watches the group at her table. There is dismay. No one knows the second name of the author of Peter Pan, J. M. Barrie. She walks carefully back to her seat. The barman's voice booms from the microphone, 'What is the height of Ben Nevis? Ben Nevis, Britain's highest mountain. What is its height?' There are groans and wild guesses around the table. Ivy speaks. 'Four thousand, four hundred and six . . . feet. Or at least it used to be. I went up twice. Before there were so many people up there. Maybe it's been worn away a bit . . . four thousand four hundred and six.' There is much scribbling. The next question, 'In what year did the Empire exhibition take place in Bellahouston Park in Glasgow . . . the Empire exhibition in Bellahouston Park?' The table is stunned. They look at Ivy. '1938 . . . I bought a jug with the Queen on it. Her nose was smudged.' She chuckles. The table writes. Ivy remembers something, 'Matthew. James Matthew Barrie. Go on. Write it down . . .'

Ivy has her coat off. There is an expectant hush. The barman is about to announce the results. 'The winner tonight is team number eleven. Number eleven.' Ivy's table erupts. The man sitting next to her kisses Ivy. She calls, as though speaking a foreign language, 'Drinks all round. Drinks all round!'

Ivy is walking along Princes Street. She stops to talk to a beggar. The beggar takes a photograph of her. She gives him a large denomination note. This is repeated several times.

Ivy is in her sitting room seated in her chair. Every surface is covered with photographs of Ivy. From the telephone comes her son's voice. 'You're running through money at a tremendous rate, Ma. The last telephone bill . . . and your current account must be nearly empty. I'll put more in when I get back. Now are you sure you'll be all right? I'll be away a week.' Ivy reassures him. 'I'm fine. I've thirty pounds in my purse. And friends the world over. Off you go and enjoy yourself. Don't do anything I wouldn't do.' Her son's voice is tired, 'I won't.' Ivy speaks sharply, 'On second thoughts . . . do . . .'

Ivy is once again far beyond the suburbs, walking towards the estuary. She is dressed in the clothes of her youth. She is clutching her purse. She stands by a railing over-looking the sea. She tries to shove her purse in her pocket, misses her pocket and the purse falls into the sea. She makes a face.

*   *   *

It is dusk. Ivy is on the road by the estuary approaching a bus stop. She looks through her pockets. Five pence. She starts to trudge towards Granton, warily. A car comes along and she ducks behind a tree.

In Ivy's sitting room son, doctor and a police constable are having a conference. The doctor speaks. 'No one's seen her for three days. It may be nothing. Everything seems in order.' The son is silent. The constable says his piece: 'We've searched the house. There's no money anywhere. Should there be?' The son shakes himself. 'I was keeping an eye. She was spending a fortune.' As he speaks he is dialling the bank. A disembodied voice answers, 'Bank of Scotland. Can I help you?' 'Derek Primrose here. Can you tell me if my mother has made any withdrawals in the last three days?' 'One minute . . . No, none at all since we last spoke to you. The account has been empty since the end of the month. Can we do anything?' 'No, thank you. I'll be in touch.' There is silence. Then the doctor speaks: 'Is it possible she's out there somewhere with no money? Where would she go if she had no money?' The son sits up.

The son and the police clamber over rocks in the lee of Granton pier. Tucked away in a corner out of sight, Ivy is barely breathing.

Ivy and son emerge from Ivy's house. He is carrying a suitcase. The car at the kerb is packed with her belongings. Ivy is dressed neatly in beige. The son locks the door. Ivy walks slowly towards the car. She is very frail. She turns to look at the house. 'Will you take me one last time to Granton pier?'

The car is parked at the far end of the pier facing out to sea. Son and mother look out over the Forth. The son is convincing himself that they are doing the right thing, 'They'll look after you well. And you'll be close by. You'll be allowed out whenever you want . . . whenever they have someone free to go with you . . . there are some nice parks in North London . . . and you'll be safe . . .' Ivy looks at him with love. 'I know, son. I've thought a lot about it. That's all right. You're a good, good son to me.' She gazes out to sea . . . 'Will you take a photograph of me sitting here in the car? To remind me?' She turns, holding out her camera. 'Just one?' He climbs out of the car. When he is some yards away she calls to him, 'Son, buy yourself a new car. A really smart fast car. Red.' He calls over his shoulder, 'I've got a car.'

Her son moves further and further away to get the whole car in the frame. He clambers up a bollard. When he turns he raises the camera. Through the lens he sees the car start to move. It gathers speed. The camera clicks. The car sails above the sea. Ivy is smiling for the camera.

A SHARED
EXPERIENCE

Paula Fitzpatrick

I suppose I got on Margaret's nerves right from the start – but then she was one of those wee lassies on a very tight wire, if you know what I mean. Anyway, there I was in the TV lounge in the Southern General maternity wing, just staring into space, keeping myself to myself and I didn't hear her properly the first time so she had to repeat the question and that annoyed her.

'Ah'm sayin', whit time do YOU make it?' she said. Loudly.

I glanced at my watch.

'Nearly half-past.'

'WHIT? Whit did ye say?' she shouted. She threw up an arm towards the wall clock. 'Is that thing right, right enough? They' – a nod towards the empty doorway – 'they wis tellin' me it's fast.'

We were quite alone in the room and she was leaning forward on her seat, staring at me with a look of outrage on her face as if she had caught me in a lie and intended to take matters further. That was when it first occurred to me that being pregnant is no guarantee of being sane – far from it. And she looked far from it to me at that moment. She also looked too young to have left school yet.

'Well, actually, I make it just after twenty-five past,' I admitted.

'Half-past's visitin'. Ye said half-past,' she complained.

But a lot of the tension seemed to have gone out of her as suddenly as it had come. She eased herself to her feet. There must have been only about eight stone of her, nearly a third of which was pregnancy. A striped hospital dressing gown was belted over her bulging middle, a hem of pink nightie showed under the candlewick gown and legs like two white matchsticks ended in fluffy, clip-clop slippers. With her long, centre-parted dark hair hanging like rats' tails over her face, she was some sight. Mind you, I wasn't feeling exactly glamorous myself.

She crossed the room and joined me companionably on the couch, sitting so close that the child in her womb could have kicked the child in mine.

'Are ye havin' visitors?' she asked.

'Not tonight.'

My husband had only just brought me to the hospital, driving in through an August downpour so heavy the windscreen wipers could hardly cope. I told her about it just to have something to say, described myself waddling like a duck across the car park in the rain, wondering how on earth I was supposed to follow Andrew's instructions and 'make a run for it' in my state. I had hoped to make her laugh but all I got was a pitying look and a knowing nod.

'Dumped you and buggered off home, has he?'

It wasn't quite how I would have put it but it was close enough. She took another look at me and grinned for the first time.

'Ye're certainly too bliddy late tae make a run fur it noo.'

I patted my bump and agreed. 'About nine and a half months too late, pet.'

We both laughed.

'See me?' she said, suddenly serious again. 'See when Ah get oot o' here? Ah'm aff! Ah never asked fur this, never wanted it.'

I saw her searching my face for a reaction to this statement – outrage, admiration, anything – but I kept blank and silent. Well, what can you say? Just a kid herself so she was.

'He's wantin' to marry me, Boyce is. That's his mother's idea. Next thing ye know Ah'll be knocked up again. Well, Ah'm no' havin' it. Ah'll make a run fur it OK, you wait an' see. She kin huv the wean. Pair o' heid-bangers, him an' his ma! Got a fag?'

The only decoration on the walls around us was a huge poster warning of the dangers of nicotine. I tried not to let my gaze stray towards it as I shook my head.

'Sorry, I don't smoke.'

She tossed her hair back and narrowed her eyes in my direction.

'Ah'm gaspin' fur wan.'

'Sorry.'

'Boyce is comin'. He'll no' bring me any fags though. Says it's bad fur the wean. Cheap bastard. Whit aboot me?'

She was on her feet again, restless and ungainly, shuffling around the room as if looking for some means of escape. I left her there. I got out when she wasn't looking, beat it to the safety of my bed and my magazine and hid from the other patients' visitors behind a copy of *My Weekly*, hoping no Good Samaritan would come across me. She'd unnerved me, that girl. I wanted a bit of peace and quiet.

But just as I was starting to relax, I caught a movement out of the corner of my eye and she appeared, wandering the ward, her hair newly brushed and pigtailed over one shoulder, her eyes blank. She made straight for me.

'Ah'm supposed to be in bed. Visitin' times ye're always

supposed to be in bed. If that old bat catches me here Ah'll get jip. In bed durin' visitin', that's the rules. Whit's the point though, eh? Whit's it matter?'

What could I say? I wanted to tell her not to make trouble for herself, not in here, but I knew she wouldn't understand.

She stood in silence for a few moments, looking across my bed and out of the window. Finally, without asking, she took the magazine from my hand and flipped absent-mindedly through the pages.

'When are ye due?' she asked.

'Last week. I'm going to be induced tomorrow.'

'Oh aye? That's good. Ah've bin here three weeks an' they've no' given me a date yet.'

It began to look as if we might get a conversation going after all but our timing was wrong.

'Magrit!'

At the threshold of the four-bed bay, a man hovered shyly. Boyce, I supposed. Shaved head, black vest displaying tattooed arms, he was aged somewhere between seventeen and fifty. All eyes fixed themselves on him. All eyes except hers. She stood with her back to him, not hearing.

'Magrit!'

When she still did not respond, I politely drew her attention to her visitor and she turned and glared at him.

'Whit kept ye? Whit ur ye standin' there fur?'

Her habit of firing questions seemed to have an even worse effect on him than it did on me. His face worked over as if he were trying to communicate with her through his eyeballs – sans use of mouth.

She stared him down, punishing him for his lateness and he was forced to speak, though nearly choking on self-consciousness.

'Whit ur ye doin' up this end? Ye're never at yer own bed! Whit dae ye keep wanderin' aboot fur?'

She ignored this and summoned him into the bay with a twitch of her head and they moved down to the chairs beside the window to conduct their visit while I retreated back behind my magazine.

They kept their voices low, her questions, his answers. The more she talked, the more he grunted and nodded. There was no doubt about who was laying down the law – much good might it do her! I had a sudden image in my mind of Andrew, an hour since, standing in the hospital corridor with my empty suitcase, nodding away while some hard-faced wee nurse gave him his orders, telling him when I'd be taken down to the labour suite and not to come in too early because nothing much would be happening for an hour or two. She didn't want him getting bored. Bored? Doesn't your heart bleed for the menfolk? As soon as she turned away, I got him by the throat (in a manner of speaking) and told him when I wanted him in. And never mind about being bored! And he went right on nodding and agreeing. I knew well enough that when the morning came, he would show up whenever he thought best – no matter what anyone else said.

I tried to blot out their conversation, Margaret's and Boyce's, but it wasn't easy and I heard the end-of-visit bell with relief. Before he left, Boyce reached into the jacket he'd been carrying. Never mind flowers and chocolates though, this man knew where his woman lived! He'd brought her a piece and jam wrapped in the wax paper from a Mother's Pride loaf. Margaret fell on the thing as if she hadn't seen food in a week. By the time I'd slipped out of bed, heading for a bath and the privacy of a locked door, she had strawberry jelly ear to ear and a look of childlike contentment on her face.

Our paths did not cross again for three days. An eternity in maternity.

It was well into the evening and visiting had just finished and I was on the hunt for the fresh nappies kept in the store behind the nurses' desk. That was when I saw her. She was eating again. Someone had brought her a bag of oranges and she was sitting on the end of her bed surrounded by orange peel. The air reeked of the fruit. She had no knife and her fingernails were bitten to the quick so how she was managing was a mystery to me but juice ran down her chin and neck and her hands were covered in a sticky mess. On the white bedspread, a yellow stain had spread around discarded peel.

I didn't intend to stop, but my stitches had slowed me down and she looked up and our eyes met and I realized with a start that she wasn't pregnant any more. So what could I do? I had to be polite. I mean, we knew each other, didn't we? We'd talked, built bridges across the Govan/Mosspark divide. Above all, we had a shared experience now, motherhood. What's more, I was two kids further down the line than she was, I had a lot of advice to offer this girl – always supposing she'd changed her mind about giving the baby up.

I smiled and got that unblinking, blank stare in response. Same old Magrit. I thought of Boyce and wondered if he had been responsible for the oranges. I tried to picture them as a family, the kid growing up, maybe going to school with my own child.

'You've had your baby then. Boy or girl?' I asked.

Without taking her eyes off me she lifted a chunk of orange to her mouth and began to work the flesh from the skin with her teeth. I shuffled across to the crib and leaned over, causing an immediate wail from the baby which made me recoil with embarrassment. I straightened up and smiled at Margaret apologetically but she let her gaze drop just long enough to reach for another orange then, watching me closely again, she broke the peel with her teeth and began tearing the thing apart with her blunt fingertips.

The wail from the crib rose in a crescendo but neither of us moved.

'Could he be hungry?' I ventured.

She spoke at last then, but her mouth was full of orange so it was hard to make out what she was saying. Only two words came across clearly, '. . . bugger off . . .'

Bridges are flimsy things and motherhood guarantees absolutely nothing. I felt we'd run out of chit-chat, Margaret and I, so I left.

FLIGHT OF FANCY

G. A. Pickin

I strained my eyes, searching amongst the river's boulders for a sign of movement, willing him to be there. I'd seen him every single day for the last three weeks, once I got to know his territory. After a few chance sightings I began timing his habits so that I wouldn't miss him.

But two days ago I couldn't find the heron anywhere, nor yesterday, nor today. I realized I was clenching my fists, digging my stubby fingernails into my lined, unlovely hands, repeating 'He must be here, he must be here' over and over under my breath like a prayer. It seemed that whichever deity watched over me, and over herons, had defected to the other side.

I searched the sky, looking upstream, the direction he inevitably chose for his morning flight. You can't mistake him for any of the other birds that inhabit the riverside. He's so free and solitary, never darting or swooping but travelling in a long, gentle glide full of quiet dignity. The pale, almost bluish colour of his underparts as he flies over always reminds me of my own eyes when I was young.

'Neither grey nor blue,' my ma used to say, 'but full of promise.'

Like my heron. I've got to the point now where it's a matter of survival. Somehow, no matter what mood I was in when I came out for my walk, everything is put right if he's there. I know it's silly, and childish, and impossible, but when I catch sight of him, even if it's only for a moment, I can feel something lifting inside me.

I can't believe I even tried to explain it to Jim. He was cleaning his rifle when I told him, polishing the already gleaming stock with his special gun rag. He keeps them locked up, 'out of harm's way', he says, although he means out of *my* way, as if I could ever want the use of them.

'Like a lucky mascot, this heron?' he asked me.

Although it's not really what I meant, I agreed. He probably never needs to escape from himself, the way I do, so he wouldn't understand how important the heron is to me.

'Where did you say you saw him?' Jim now gave me his full attention, using that keen look he gets when he thinks he's striking a shrewd deal with some tourist in the shop.

'Along the pebble beach, and upstream by the little island,' I told him. I saw him narrow his eyes and nod slightly. 'Why?'

'Because this may be our lucky break, Ailsa. Mr McBride from the George Hotel is turning his function room into a posh restaurant. He wants to call it "The Heron", and serve exotic fish dishes at jumped-up prices. He's asked me if I can do him a stuffed heron.'

'You can't,' I clutched at his arm, pleading with him. 'Not my heron, not my lucky heron.'

'You'll be able to see him whenever you want, once they've put him in a glass case. I've never done anything with a long neck. It will be quite a challenge.'

I opened my mouth to protest, the tears of anger and frustration coursing down my face. But Jim gave me one of his warning looks.

'Ailsa, no nonsense. The price is right.'

I knew then what a terrible mistake I'd made, and, after my unwitting betrayal, it was up to him to survive Jim's gun for as long as his heron's wits would serve him.

Although I tried to keep an eye on what Jim brought in with him after each hunting trip, it was impossible to catch him every time. I was too busy serving customers, fetching dried peas off the top shelf or rummaging through the drawers behind the counter for fishing line or shotgun shells.

Jim and I had taken over the shop when a hunting accident put paid to his job on the ferry. I admit that his idea to turn half the space over to fishing equipment and hunting accessories had been a smart move, for the 'leisure' side of the business turned out to be the most lucrative.

But then Jim got this bright idea of stuffing 'trophies'. He got a grant and learned off a man in Dumfries, travelling down on Tuesdays and Thursdays, bringing back road kills, dead pets, anything he could use to practise on. I've got to hand it to him, he's quite good at it now, and lots of the locals and a fair number of tourists make use of his skills, adorning their dens with the stuffed skins of creatures they have murdered. Or 'bagged', as they put it.

He's done a range of game birds – grouse, pheasant, pigeon, even a ptarmigan. As for me, I won't even have cut flowers in the house. I see nothing decorative or nostalgic in filling a room with dead things.

The whole idea of my heron, filled with wire and kapok, or whatever it is Jim uses, made me feel physically sick. The shiny glass eyes gazing sightlessly from within a glass box would make him look stupid, witless. And after the novelty wore off, the patrons of the George would cease to notice him. Perhaps Mr McBride would think up a new theme for his restaurant, or move on to some other pub, consigning the heron to a storeroom somewhere, where mould and insects would take their toll. The poor bird won't even have served the fleeting purpose of providing someone with a full belly.

All those people who will see his dead form won't know him as I know him. His slow-motion flight and awkward body camouflage a master fisherman. When they see that distinctive crest on his head, glued into place, they won't be able to appreciate the speed and grace his neck had as he caught his prey.

'Model your movements on the swan,' my ma had advised me, inspecting my own long, gangly limbs. But I'm sure she would have included the heron in her advice, had she ever seen one. Not raucous nor flamboyant, just quietly competent, that's the heron.

But today, I couldn't find him anywhere. Not up the creek, or by the island, or round the bend by the old mill. Even though I know it might be coincidence, I also know that Jim's been busy in his workroom these last three days. I haven't had the nerve to go in and see what he's up to, although he's been humming and singing all round the shop when he can spare the time to help with the serving. Instead, I've haunted the riverbank, hoping to get a glimpse and put my heart at rest.

I headed back up the lane, past the holiday cottages and the village green, down the little path by the church into Drove Road, where the shop is. And there they were. Mr McBride and Jim, standing in the doorway, shaking hands, big smiles on both their faces showing lots of even gleaming white teeth, their arms pumping and pumping as they congratulated each other on a deal well made. I stopped for a moment in the shadow of the church, and felt my insides go cold and hollow the way they do when you're anticipating the worst, and lose that last warm kernel of hope inside.

Then, something took over inside of me. I gathered my spindly legs beneath me, ran in long loping steps, and pushed past the two men, breaking through the clasped hands and the nodding heads. I dashed through the shop and back into Jim's workroom, flinging the door wide with a bang and slamming on the light switch. The room was a mass of wire and feathers, and gave off an odour of glue, chemicals, and offal. But my heron wasn't there. The two men were still staring into the shop, wondering what had hit them, when I flew out again, straight to the van at the kerb, with the big green and gold logo of the George painted on the side. The rear doors were unlocked, and I wrenched them open, my arms flung wide with the effort as if to embrace the contents of the van. There on the cold metal floor was a box, a crate really, just the right size for a heron's coffin. I must have screamed, because Jim was shaken into action then. I could feel him trying to restrain me as I ripped off the lid of the crate, my fingers catching and tearing on the rough wood and cheap staples.

And there he was, sighted at last. He was resting calmly on his side in a bed of Excelsior, gutted and stuffed. Not my heron, but the skin of my heron, crude and dead, with those dopey glass eyes staring out at me. His shape was unnaturally thin, and the once-graceful neck was slightly lumpy, as if he'd caught a fish down his throat in mid-swallow. I shook off Jim's fingers and grabbed up the mutilated corpse, heading back the way I had come, towards the river.

Jim and Mr McBride followed me, but even with my awkward burden I outdistanced them. The heron was light, and I let my gawky legs use their length, so long kept in check, stretching out to cover the distance in even, fluid strides. I was strong too. My daily rambles have built up the muscles, while Jim's have become weak, standing in the shop or at his workbench all day. God only knows what exercise Mr McBride may get, but it doesn't include his lungs, for he soon stopped, doubled up and panting, before he even reached the edge of the wood.

With the inner compass that guides a hunted animal, my legs took me through the hedge at a thin spot, and I scrambled up the bank. I ignored the brambles, letting them rake and catch along my clothing and skin, but being careful to keep my heron high above the lethal thorns. Then I found his tree.

This is the tree where he and his mate had their nest last season. I climbed up, using my sweater to tie the heron to my back as best I could. Higher and higher, then out over the river, to the same fork where the nest lies, empty now, waiting for the next season's eggs.

So here I sit with my heron, his glass eyes gazing into mine, waiting to see what we shall do next. Jim is calling from below, shouting for me to come down, begging and threatening and screeching. He has raised the crows, and they circle above, mimicking his anger in their sarcastic way. I can see Mr McBride too, making his way down the path, his shiny shoes going matt with mud and leaves. I inch along a bit further, and let my legs dangle into space. The river's loud rushing noise drowns the human sounds, and my heron and I look out, first downstream, to the beach, then up, away towards the source of the river.

This is the way he has seen it countless times, this view high above the mud and turmoil. Perhaps he has been up into the mountains and even caught fish from the head waters.

Like an out-of-focus picture come clear, I see it. Instead of being alone, trapped in glass boxes that cramp our limbs, we could launch ourselves off this branch, my heron and I. We could spread our wings and soar away, high above the river, the village, and Jim. We would be so distant that it would take the best field glasses in the shop to make out any details of our features.

I take one last look below, and throw out my arms, my

heron beside me. We circle once, then turn upstream, our legs dangling behind us, and slowly, tantalizingly, we disappear from view.

SOUVENIRS

Leila Aboulela

They set out early, before sunset. Not the right time for
visiting, but it was going to be a long drive and his sister
Manaal said she would not be able to recognize the painter's house in the dark. The car slipped from the shaded
car-port into the white sunlight of the afternoon, the
streets were empty, their silence reminiscent of dawn.

Since he had come on the plane from Scotland two
weeks ago, Yassir had not gone out at this time of day.
Instead he had rested after lunch wearing his old *jellabia*.
He would lie on one of the beds that were against the
walls of the sitting room, playing with a toothpick in his
mouth and talking to Manaal without looking at her. On
the bed at right angles to his, she would lie with her feet
near his head so that had they been children she might
have reached out and pulled his hair with her toes. And
the child Yassir would have let his heels graze the white
wall leaving brown stains for which he would be punished
later. Now they talked slowly, probing for common
interests and so remembering things past, gossiping lightly
about others, while all the time the air cooler blew the
edges of the beds' sheets just a little, intermittently, and
the smells of lunch receded. Then the air cooler's sound
would take over, dominate the room, blowing their
thoughts away and they would sleep until the time came
when all the garden was in shade.

In this respect, Yassir had slotted easily into the life of

Khartoum. After five years on the North Sea oil rigs, noisy helicopter flights to and from Dyce airport, a grey sea with waves as crazy as the sky. Five years of two weeks offshore, two weeks on with Emma in Aberdeen. No naps after lunch there and yet he could lie here and know that the rhythms the air cooler whispered into his heart were familiar, well known. When he had first arrived he had put fresh straw into the air cooler's box. Standing outdoors on an overturned Pepsi crate, he had wedged open the grimy perforated frame with a screwdriver, unleashed cobwebs and plenty of dust. Fresh powdery dust and solid fluffs that had lost all resemblance to sand. The old bale of straw had shrunk over the years, gone dark and rigid from the constant exposure to water. He oiled the water pump and put in the new bale of straw. Its smell filled the house for days, the air that blew out was cooler. For this his mother had thanked him and like other times before, prayed that he would find only good people in his path. It was true, he was always fortunate in the connections he made, in the people who held the ability to further his interests. In the past teachers, now his boss, his colleagues, Emma.

But 'Your wife – what's her name?' was how his mother referred to Emma. She would not say Emma's name. She would not 'remember' it. It would have been the same if Emma had been Jane, Alison or Susan, any woman from 'outside'. Outside that large pool of names his mother knew and could relate to. That was his punishment, nothing more, nothing less. He accepted it as the nomad bears the times of drought which come to starve his cattle, biding time, waiting for the tightness to run its course and the rain that must eventually fall. Manaal would smile embarrassed when their mother said that. And as if time had dissolved the age gap between them, she would attempt a faint defence. 'Leave him alone, Mama,' she would say in a whisper, avoiding their eyes, wary, lest her words instead of calming, provoked the much-feared outburst. Manaal had met Emma two years ago in Aberdeen. What she had told his mother about Emma, what she had said to try to drive away the rejection that gripped her, he didn't know.

For Yassir, Emma was Aberdeen. Unbroken land after the sea. Real life after the straight lines of the oil rig. A kind of freedom. Before Emma his leave onshore had floated, never living up to his expectations. And it was essential for those who worked on the rigs that those onshore days were fulfilling enough to justify the hardship of the rigs. A certain formula was needed, a certain balance which evaded him. Until one day he visited the dentist for two fillings and, with lips frozen with procaine, read out loud the name, Emma, written in Arabic, on a golden necklace that hung around the receptionist's throat.

'Your wife – what's her name?' his mother says as if clumsily smudging out a fact, hurting it. A fact, a history. Three years ago he drove Emma to the maternity ward in Foresterhill, in the middle of a summer's night that looked like twilight, to deliver a daughter who did not make her appearance until the afternoon of the following day. Samia changed in the two weeks that he did not see her. Her growth marked time like nothing else did. Two weeks offshore, two weeks with Emma and Samia, two weeks offshore again, Emma driving him to the heliport, the child in her own seat at the back. A fact, a history. Yet here, when Manaal's friends visited, some with toddlers, some with good jobs, careers, there was a 'see what you've missed' atmosphere around the house. An atmosphere that was neither jocular nor of regret. So that he had come to realize, with the sick bleakness that accompanies truth, that his mother imagined that he could just leave Emma and leave the child, come home, and those five years would have been just an aberration, time forgotten. He could marry one of Manaal's friends, one who would not mind that he had been married before, that he had left behind a child somewhere in Europe. A bride who would regard all that as a man's experience. When talking to her friends she would say the word 'experienced' in a certain way, smiling secretly.

Because the streets were silent, Yassir and Manaal were silent too, as if by talking they would disturb those who were resting indoors. Yassir drove slowly, pebbles spat out from under the wheels, he was careful to avoid the potholes. The windows wide open let in dust but closing them would be suffocating. From their house in Safia they crossed the bridge into Khartoum and it was busier there, more cars, more people walking in the streets. That part of the journey, the entry into Khartoum, reminded him of the Blue Nile Cinema, which was a little way under the bridge. He remembered as a student walking back from the cinema, late at night to the Barracks, as his hostel was called, because it was once army barracks. He used to walk with his friends in a kind of swollen high, full of the film he had just seen. Films like *A Man for All Seasons, Educating Rita, Chariots of Fire.*

There was still a long way for them to go, past the Extension, beyond the airport, past Riyadh to the newly built areas of Taif and El-Ma'moura. Not a very practical idea, a drain of the week's ration of petrol and there was the possibility that the painter would not be in and the whole journey would have been wasted. Manaal was optimistic though. 'They'll be in,' she said, '*insha Allah.* Especially if we get there early enough before they go out anywhere.' There were no telephones in El-Ma'moura; it was a newly built area with no street numbers, no addresses.

That morning, he had mentioned buying a painting or two to take back to Aberdeen and Manaal had suggested Ronan K. He was English, his wife gave private English lessons (Manaal was once her student). Now in the car when he asked more about him she said, 'For years he sat doing nothing, he had no job, maybe he was painting. I didn't know about that until the Hilton commissioned him to do some paintings for the cafeteria. No one knows why this couple live here. They are either crazy or they are spies. Everyone thinks they are spies.'

'You all like to think these sensational things', he said. 'What is there to spy on anyway?'

'They're nice though,' she said. 'I hope they are not spies.'

Yassir shook his head, thinking it was hopeless to talk sense to her.

The paintings were not his idea, they were Emma's. Emma was good with ideas, new suggestions, it was one of the things he admired about her. Yassir didn't know much about painting. If he walked into a room he would not notice the paintings on the wall and he secretly thought they were an extravagance. But then he felt like that about many of the things Emma bought. What he considered luxuries, she considered necessities. Like the Bambi wallpaper in Samia's room must be bought to match the curtains, which match the bedspread, which match Thumper on the pillowcase. And there was a *Bambi* video, a Ladybird book, a pop-up book. He would grumble but she would persuade him. She would say that as a child she had cried in the cinema when Bambi's mother was shot. Popcorn could not stop the tears, the nasal flood. Of pop-up books and Hallowe'en costumes, she would say, as a child I had these things. He would think: I didn't.

This time Emma had asked 'What can you get from Khartoum for the house?' They were eating muesli and watching Mr Motivator on GMTV. Mr M. had a litre and a half of bottled mineral water in each hand. He was using them as weights while he squatted down and up, down and up, *Knees over your toes*. The labels on the bottles had been slyly removed.

'Nothing. There's nothing there,' Yassir said.

'What do tourists get when they go there?'

'Tourists don't go there,' he said. 'It's not a touristy place. The only foreigners there are working.' Once when Yassir was in university he had met a British journalist. The journalist was wearing shorts which looked comical because no one else wore shorts unless they were playing sports. He had chatted to Yassir and some of his friends.

'There must be something you can get,' Emma said. 'Things carved in wood, baskets . . .'

'There's a shop which sell ivory things. Elephants made of ivory and things like that.'

'No. Not ivory.'

'I could get you a handbag made of crocodile skin?'

'No, yuck.'

'Snakeskin?'

'Stop it, I'm serious.'

'Ostrich feathers?'

'NO DEAD ANIMALS. Think of something else.'

'There's a bead market. Someone once told me about that. I don't know where it is, though. I'll have to find out.'

'If you get me beads I can have them made here into a necklace.' Emma liked necklaces but not bracelets or earrings. The golden necklace with her name in Arabic was from an ex-boyfriend, a mud-logger who had been working rotational from the oil rigs in Oman.

'Change your mind and come with me. You can take the malaria pills, Samia can take the syrup and it's just a few vaccines . . .'

'A few jabs! Typhoid, yellow fever, cholera, TB! And Samia might get bitten by this sandfly Manaal told us about when she came here. She is only three. It's not worth it – maybe when she's older . . .'

'You're not curious to see where I grew up?'

'I am interested a bit but – I don't know – I've never heard anything good about that place.'

'This is just a two-week holiday, that's all. My mother will get to see you and Samia, you'll have a look around . . .' he said, switching Mr Motivator off.

'Paintings,' she said. 'That's what you should get. You can bring back paintings of all those things you think I should be curious about. Or just take lots of photographs and bring the beads.'

He bought the beads but did not take any photographs. He had shied away from that, as if unable to click a camera at his house, his old school, the cinemas that brought the sparkle of life abroad. So when Manaal said she knew this English painter, he was enthusiastic about the idea even though it was his last evening in Khartoum. Tomorrow his flight would leave for home. He hoped he would have with him some paintings for Emma. She would care about where each one went, on this wall or that. She cared about things more than he did. She even cared about Samia more than he did. Emma was in tune with the child's every burp and whimper. In comparison to Emma, Yassir's feelings for Samia were jammed up, unable to flow. Sometimes with the two of them he felt himself dispensable, he thought they could manage without him. They did just that when he was offshore. They had a life together; playgroup, kindergym, Duthie Park. When Manaal came to Aberdeen she said many times, 'Emma is so good with the child. She talks to her as if she is an adult.'

Yassir now wondered, as they drove down Airport Road,

if Manaal had said such positive things to his mother. Or if she had only told of the first day of her visit to Aberdeen. The day she reached out to hold the sleeping child and Emma said, 'No, I'd rather you didn't. She'll be frightened if she wakes up and finds a stranger holding her.' The expression on Manaal's face had lingered throughout the whole visit as she cringed in Emma's jumpers that were too loose, too big for her. Then, as if lost in the cold, his sister hibernated, slept and slept through the nights and large parts of the days. So that Emma began to say, she must be ill, there must be something wrong with her, some disease, why does she sleep so much Yassir, why? Possessive of Manaal, he had shrugged, Aberdeen's fresh air, and not explained that his sister had always been like that, easily tired, that she reacted to life's confusions by digging herself into sleep.

When they left the airport behind them and began to pass Riyadh, Manaal suddenly said that to make sure they get to the right house, she had better drop in on her friend Zahra. Zahra's mother, a Bulgarian, was a good friend of Mrs K. and they would know where the house was.

'I thought *you* knew where it is?'

'I do – but it's better to be sure. It's on our way, anyway.'

'Isn't it too early to go banging on people's doors?'

'No, it's nearly five. Anyway her parents are away – they've gone to *Hajj*.'

'Who? The Bulgarian woman? You're joking.'

'No, *wallahi.*' Manaal seemed amused by his surprise. 'Zahra's mother prays and fasts Ramadan. We were teasing her the last time I went there, telling her that when she comes back from *hajj*, she'll start covering her hair and wearing long sleeves. And she said, "No never, your country is too hot, it's an oven."' Manaal did an impersonation of grammatically incorrect Arabic with a Bulgarian accent which made Yassir laugh. He thought of Zahra's father, a man who was able to draw his foreign wife to Islam, and Yassir attributed to him qualities of strength and confidence.

The house, in front of which Manaal told him to stop, had a high wall around it. The tops of the trees that grew inside fell over the wall, shading the pavement. Manaal banged on the metal door – there was no bell. She banged with her palms, and peered through the chink in the door to see if anyone was coming.

Yassir opened the car door to let in some air but there was hardly any breeze. There were tears in the plastic of Manaal's seat from which bits of yellow foam protruded. There was a crack in the window, fine and long, like a map of the Nile, and one of the doors in the back was stuck and could never be opened. This car, he thought would not pass its MOT in Aberdeen, it would not be deemed roadworthy. What keeps it going here is *baraka*.

The car had seen finer days in his father's lifetime. Then it was solid and tinged with prestige. Now, more than anything else, its decay was proof of the passing of time, the years of Yassir's absence. He had suggested to his mother and Manaal that he should buy them a new one. Indeed this had been one of the topics of his stay – a new car – the house needs fixing – parts of the garden wall are crumbling away – why don't you get out of this dump and move to a new house? But his mother and sister tended to put up with things. Like with Manaal recently losing her job. She had worked since graduation with a Danish aid agency, writing reports in their main office in Souk Two. When they had reduced their operations in the south, staff cuts followed. 'Start looking for a new job,' he told her, 'or have you got certain plans that I don't know of yet?' She laughed and said, 'When you leave I'll start looking for a job and no, there are no certain plans. There is no one on the horizon yet.'

It was a joke between them. There is no one on the horizon yet. She wrote this at the bottom of letters, letters in Arabic that Emma could not read. Year after year. She was twenty-five now and he could feel the words touched by the frizzle of anxiety. 'Every university graduate is abroad, making money so that he can come back and marry a pretty girl like you,' he had said recently to her. 'Really?' she replied with a sarcasm that was not characteristic of her.

From the door of Zahra's house, Manaal looked at Yassir in the car and shrugged, then banged again with both hands. But she must have heard someone coming for she raised her hand to him and nodded.

The girl who opened the door had a towel wrapped around her hair like a turban. She kissed Manaal and he could hear, amidst their greetings, the words shower and sorry. They walked towards him, something he was not expecting and before he could get out of the car the girl leaned and, through the open window of the seat next to his, extended her hand. The car filled up with the smell of soap and shampoo; he thought his hand would later smell of her soap. She had the same colouring as his daughter, Samia, the froth of cappuccino, dark grey eyes, thick eyebrows. Her face was dotted with pink spots, round and raised like little sweets. He imagined those grey eyes soft with sadness when she examined her acne in the bathroom mirror, running her fingertips over the bumps.

With a twig and some pebbles, Zahra drew them a map of the painter's house in the dust of the pavement. She sat on her heels rather primly, careful not to get dust on her *jellabia*. She marked the main road and where they should turn left. When you see a house with no garden walls, no fence, she said, that's where you should turn left.

She stood up, dusted off her hands and when Manaal got into the car, she waved to them until they turned and were out of sight. Yassir drove back onto the main road, from the dust to the asphalt. The asphalt road was raised and because it had no pavements, its sides were continually being eroded, eaten away. They looked jagged, crumbly. The afternoon was beginning to mellow, sunset was drawing near.

'I imagine that when Samia grows up she will look like your friend,' he said.

'Maybe, yes. I haven't thought of it before,' Manaal said. 'Did you like the earrings for Samia?'

He nodded. His mother had given him a pair of earrings for Samia. He had thanked her and not said that his daughter's ears were not pierced.

'She's beginning to accept the situation.' His voice had a tinge of bravado about it. He was talking about his mother and Manaal knew. She was looking out of the window. She turned to him and said, 'She likes the photographs that you send. She shows them to everyone.'

Yassir had been sending photographs from Aberdeen. Photographs of Emma and Samia. Some were in the snow, some taken in the Winter Gardens at Duthie Park, some at home.

'So why doesn't she tell me that? Instead of "What's her name?" or whatever she keeps saying?'

'You should have given her some idea very early on, you should have . . . consulted her.' Manaal spoke slowly, with caution, like she was afraid or just tired.

'And what would she have said if I had asked her? Tell me, what do you think she would have said?'

'I don't know.'

'You do know.'

'How can I?'

'She would have said no, and then what?'

'I don't know. I just know that it was wrong to suddenly write a letter and say "I got married" – in the past tense. Nobody does that.'

He didn't answer her. He did not like the hurt in her voice, like it was her own hurt not their mother's.

As if his silence disturbed her and she wanted the conversation to continue she said, 'It wasn't kind.'

'It was honest.'

'But it was hard. She was like someone ill when she read your letter. Defeated and ill . . .'

'She'll come to accept it.'

'Of course she'll come to accept it. That's the whole point. It's inevitable but you could have made it easier for her, that's all.' Then in a lighter tone she said, 'Do something theatrical. Get down on your knees and beg for her forgiveness.'

They laughed at this together, somewhat deliberately to ease the tension. What he wanted to do was explain, speak about Emma and say: She welcomed me, I was on the periphery and she let me in. Do people get tortured to death in that dentist's chair or was I going to be the first? he had asked Emma that day, and made her smile, when he stumbled out of pain and spoke to her with lips numb with procaine.

'It would have been good if Emma and Samia had come with you,' Manaal was saying.

'I wanted that too.'

'Why didn't they?' She had asked that question before, as had others. He gave different reasons to different people. Now in the car he felt that Manaal was asking deliberately, wanting him to tell her the truth. Could he say that from this part of the world Emma wanted malleable pieces, not the random whole? She desired frankincense from The Body Shop, tahina safe in a supermarket container.

'She has fears,' he said.

'What fears?'

'I don't know. The sandfly, malaria ... Some rubbish like that.' He felt embarrassed and disloyal.

They heard the sunset *azan* when they began to look for the house without a garden wall which Zahra had told them about. But there were many houses like that – people built their homes and ran out of money by the time it came to build the garden wall. So they turned left off the asphalt road anyway when they reached El-Ma'moura, hoping that Manaal would be able to recognize the street or the house.

'Nothing looks familiar to you?' he asked.

'But everything looks different than the last time I was here,' she said, 'all those new houses, it's confusing.'

There were no roads, just tracks made by previous cars, hardly any pavements. They drove through dust and stones. The houses in various stages of construction stood in straight lines. In some parts the houses formed a square around a large empty area, as if marking a place which would always be empty, where houses would not be allowed to be built.

'Maybe it's this house,' Manaal said. He parked, they rang the bell but it was the wrong house.

Back in the car they drove through the different tracks and decided to ask around. How many foreigners were living in this area anyway? People were bound to know them.

Yassir asked a fat man sitting in front of his house, one knee against his chest, picking his toenails. Near him an elderly man was praying, using a newspaper as a mat.

The man didn't seem to know but he gave Yassir several elaborate suggestions.

Yassir asked some people who were walking past but again they didn't know. This was taking a long time as everyone he asked seemed willing to engage him in conversation.

'It's your turn,' he said to Manaal when they saw a woman coming out of her house.

She went towards the woman and stood talking to her. Sunset was nearly over by then, the western sky, the houses, the dusty roads were all one colour, like the flare that burns off the rig, he thought. Manaal stood, a dark silhouette against red and brick. One hand reached out to hold her hair from blowing and her thin elbows made an angle with her head and neck through which the light came. This is what I would paint, Yassir thought, if I knew how, I would paint Manaal like this, with her elbows sticking out against the setting sun.

When she came back she seemed pleased, 'We're nearly there,' she said. 'That woman knew them. First right, and it's the second house.'

As soon as they turned right, Manaal recognized the one-storey house with the blue gate. She got out before him and rang the bell.

Ronan K. was older than Yassir had imagined. He looked like a football coach, overweight yet deft in his movements. The light from the lamp near the gate made him look slightly bald. He recognized Manaal, and as they stepped into a large bare courtyard while he closed the gate behind them, she launched into a long explanation of why they had come and how they had nearly got lost on the way.

The house inside had no tiles on the floors, its surface was of uneven textured stone, giving it the appearance that it was unfinished, still in the process of being built.

Yet the furniture was arranged in an orderly way, and there were carpets on the floor. Birds rustled in a cage near the kitchen door. On one of the walls there was a painting of the back of a woman in a *tobe*, balancing a basket on her head.

'One of yours?' Yassir asked but Ronan said no, he did not like to hang his own paintings in the house.

'All my work is on the roof,' he said, and from the kitchen got a tray with a plastic jug full of *kerkadeh* and ice and three glasses. Some of the ice splashed into the glasses as he began to pour, and a pool of redness gathered in the tray, sliding slowly around in large patterns.

'You have a room on the roof?' Yassir asked.

'That's where I paint,' Ronan said. 'I lock it though, we've had many *haramiah* in the area. Not that they would steal my paintings but it's better to be careful. I'm in there most nights though, the *kahrabah* permitting.'

Hearing the Arabic words for thieves and electricity made Yassir smile. He remembered Manaal copying the way Zahra's mother spoke. He wondered how well Ronan K. knew Arabic.

'My wife has the key. But she is right next door. The neighbours' daughter had a baby last week. There's a party of some kind there,' and he looked at Manaal as if for an explanation.

'A *simayah*,' she said.

'That's right,' said Ronan, 'a *simayah*. Maybe you could go over and get the key from her? It's right next door.'

'Is it Amina and her people? I've seen them here before,' Manaal asked him.

'Yes, that's them.'

'Last time I was here, Amina walked in with chickens to put in your freezer. There wasn't enough room in theirs.'

'Chickens with their heads still on them and all the insides,' said Ronan. 'Terrible ... This morning she brought over a leg of lamb,' and he gestured vaguely towards the kitchen.

'So who had the baby?' Manaal asked.

'Let's see if I can get this one right,' he said, 'The sister of Amina's husband, who happens to be – just to get things complicated – married to the cousin of Amina's mother.'

They laughed because Ronan gave an exaggerated sigh as if he had done a lot of hard work.

'I thought you said it was the neighbours' daughter,' said Yassir.

'Well, this Amina character,' he said, and Manaal laughed and nodded at the word 'character', 'she is living with her in-laws, so it is really the in-laws' house.'

Manaal got up to go and Ronan said, 'I'll tell you what. Just throw the keys up to us on the roof. We'll wait for you there. It will save time.'

The roof was dark and cool, its floor more uneven than that of the house had been. The ledge all around it was low, only knee-high. El-Ma'moura lay spread out before them, the half-built houses surrounded by scaffolding, the piles of sand and discarded bricks. Shadows of stray dogs made their way through the rubble. Domes of cardboard marked the places where the caretakers of the houses and their families lived. Their job was to guard the bags of cement, the toilets, the tiles that came for the new houses. Once the houses were built they would linger, drawing water from the pipes that splashed on the embyronic streets, until they were eventually sent away.

From the house next door came the sounds of children playing football, scuffling, names called out loud. A woman's voice shrieked from indoors. Yassir and Ronan sat on the ledge. He offered Yassir a cigarette and Yassir accepted though he hadn't smoked for several years. Ronan put his box of matches between them. It had a picture of a crocodile on it, mouth wide open, tail arched up in the air. Yassir had forgotten how good it felt to strike a match, flick grey ash away. It was one of the things he and Emma had done together – given up smoking.

'A long way from Aberdeen, or rather Aberdeen is a long way from here,' Ronan said.

'Have you been there before?'

'I know it well, my mother originally came from Elgin. They can be a bit parochial up there, don't you think?'

At the back of Yassir's mind questions formed themselves, rose out of a sense of habit, but drooped languidly as if there were no fuel to vocalize them. What was this man doing here, in a place where even the nights were hot and alcohol was forbidden? Where there was little comfort and little material gain? The painter sat on his roof and, like the raised spots on Zahra's face, did not arouse in Yassir derision, only passive wonder.

'If you look this way,' Ronan said, 'you can see the airport – where the red and blue lights are. Sometimes I see the airplanes circling and landing. They pass right over me when they take off. I see the fat bellies of planes full of people going away.

'Last August we had so much rain. This whole area was flooded – we couldn't drive to the main road. The Nile rose and I could see it with my telescope – even though it is far from here.'

'How long have you been here?' Yassir asked.

'Fifteen years.'

'That's a long time.'

Giant wisps of white brushed the sky as if the smoke from their cigarettes had risen high, expanded and stood still. Stars were pushing their way into view, gathering around them the darkest dregs of night. On the roof, speaking Emma's language for the first time in two weeks, Yassir missed her, not with the light eagerness he had known on the rigs but with something else, something plain and unwanted; the grim awareness of distance. He knew why he had wanted her to come with him, not to 'see', but so that the place would move her, startle her, touch her in some irreversible way.

Manaal threw up the keys, Ronan opened the locked room and put the light on. It was a single bulb which dangled from the ceiling, speckled with the still bodies of black insects. The room smelled of paint, a large fan stood in the corner. Conscious of his ignorance, Yassir was silent as Ronan, cigarette drooping from his mouth, showed him one painting after the other. 'I like them,' he said and it was true. They were clear and uncluttered, the colours light, giving an impression of sunlight. Most were of village scenes, mud houses, one of children playing with a goat, one of a tree that had fallen into the river.

'Paper is my biggest problem,' said Ronan, 'The brushes and paints last for quite some time. But if I know someone who is going abroad I always ask them for paper.'

'Is it special paper that you need?'

'Yes, thicker for watercolours.'

'I like the one of the donkey in front of the mud house,' said Yassir.

'The Hilton don't seem to want mud houses.'

'Did they tell you that?'

'No, I just got this feeling.'

'That means I could get them at a discount?'

'Maybe . . . how many were you thinking of taking?'

Yassir chose three, one of them the children with the goat because he thought Samia might like that. He paid after some haggling. Downstairs the birds were asleep in their cage, there was no longer any ice in the jug of *kerkadeh*. Manaal was waiting for him by the gate. She had a handful of dates from next door which she offered to Ronan and Yassir. The dates were dry and cracked uncomfortably under Yassir's teeth before softening into sweetness. It was now time to leave. He shook hands with Ronan. The visit was a success, he had achieved what he came for.

Manaal slept in the car on the way home. Yassir drove through streets busier than the ones he had found in the afternoon. This was his last day in Khartoum. Tomorrow night a plane would take him to Paris, another plane to Glasgow then the train to Aberdeen. Perhaps Ronan K. would be on his roof tomorrow night, watching Air France rise up over the new houses of El-Ma'moura.

The city was acknowledging his departure, recognizing his need for a farewell. Headlamps of cars jerked in the badly lit streets, thin people in white floated like clouds. Voices, rumbling lorries, trucks leaning to one side snorting fumes. On a junction with a busier road, a small bus went past carrying a wedding party. It was lighted inside, an orange light that caught the singing faces, the clapping hands. Ululations, the sound of a drum, lines from a song. Yassir drove on and gathered around him what he would take back with him, the things he could not deliver. Not the beads, not the paintings, but other things. Things devoid of the sense of their own worth. Manaal's silhouette against the rig's flare, against a sky dyed with *kerkadeh*. The scent of soap and shampoo in his car, a man picking his toenails, a page from a newspaper spread out as a mat. A voice that said, I see the planes circling at night, I see their lights ... all the people going away. Manaal saying, you could have made it easier for her, you could have been more kind.

TANGERINES

Beatrice Colin

When I was young I used to walk everywhere backwards. Just to make sure I wasn't missing anything. I still do sometimes. But now I bang into walls. One day I turned round and looked in front of me. And I was poor. And I was older and I was here.

Here, washing up in a tiny kitchen in a pink dressing gown, my hair not blonde but sort of pale yellow, my voice once sweet, now salty, my face not fresh, but dulled. Change used to be on my side. Success was my middle name. Music was my life. Clichés were my speciality. It would be funny if it wasn't all so true. I light a cigarette.

Steph's been in the bath for over an hour. You know, I can see him in my mind from here. He's drinking a bottle of beer and smoking a cigarette. The ash falls on the bath mat. The mat is still damp from the last bath he had. It still smells of stale socks and boiled cabbage.

Steph spends hours in the bath now. He just lies there like a huge great fat whale, sloshing about. But he still doesn't smell clean. The alcohol seeps through his pores.

You see, Steph was my guitar player. He organised me, helped me write the songs, sometimes picked the hits and tucked me up in bed. But now I cook for him, I iron, wash his clothes and scrub the ring off the bath. We've swapped.

Tonight we have a gig. It's just a small café which sells overpriced sandwiches to underage drinkers, nothing

189

special. But I remember the sound of my voice in the big places, clubs, halls, even the Royal Albert Hall. It seemed to echo like an angel. But that was then. Now it's twenty quid and a free sandwich.

Aah, Steph's pulling himself out of the bath. First the squeak of his flesh against the plastic and then the crump as he steps heavily on to the bath mat. I put the cigarette out and open a window. When I turn round, he's standing here in my kitchen making a puddle on the lino. His hair is slicked back with water and his belly hangs loose.

'I've had it,' he says.

'You've had what,' I reply.

'We can't go on like this,' he says. 'It's gone. It's like the glue's not there anymore.'

'I know,' I say quietly.

I stand and look out of the window at the cars racing along the motorway. It's rush hour and they line from bonnet to bumper like shiny, gaudy beads. He goes into the bedroom and puts on that ridiculous bow tie he wears to play the piano. He looks so silly now. Not what he he was.

'Your jacket's in the cupboard,' I say.

'Well done,' he replies. 'I hung it there.'

'Shall I wear my green or my pink?'

'I don't care. Whatever.'

'But do you think the pink suits me? I've never been too sure. Does it make me look fat?'

He doesn't reply. I stand there holding the dresses on the hanger. He ignores me.

'We should have . . . ,' I say.

'Why do you bring that up. That's got nothing to do with it now,' he says.

'We were so happy then,' I whisper.

'No, we weren't. We weren't happy, sad or anything. We were in orbit most of the time.'

'I knew it was the wrong . . .'

SHUT UP . . . right. Shut up. I can't stand it when you go on.'

'How can we be like we were?'

'We can't. It's past history. This is all there is.'

That night we play in the café. Three couples sit having a meal. No one claps at the end of the songs except the manager. It's dismal.

We both lie in bed later back to back. He's awake, I can tell by his breathing. His spine digs into my kidneys. Drafts whisk under the covers. I feel lonelier than a desert. It's so unfair.

You see, I can't forget. I really tried. I tried to push the past away and the more I did, the more vivid it became. Until it felt so bright, like neon in the dusk, like a roller coaster at Morecambe beach, that it didn't seem like me anymore. And I almost could invent another beginning and another ending where it all turns out fine. But you can't take things back. Because although those days were thrilling, wonderful, better than sex, they went past so fast that I lost my grip. And I was tossed about, from note to note, from night club to night club, from town to town, from year to year, from man to man. I did things I shouldn't have. And now I've got a hole, right here. And it's letting in the wind.

When I wake up, Steph has gone. Today is my birthday. I'm thirty-four. Tears fall on to the pillow until it's soaked right through. On both sides. It's time, I decide. I've waited too long. And so I put on my best dress and shove my hair up in a bun. It makes me look more respectable and hides the bleach and the roots. And then I go into the bank and withdraw all my savings. We were going to buy a little flat of our own. What's the point of having it now, I say to the woman in the bank. She doesn't appear to hear me. Next I go and hire a car. The smallest one they've got, for the weekend, is quite cheap. But it's orange. Tangerine they call it. I hate that colour, but never mind. I take it and then I drive to the suburbs.

I turn off the main road and steer down a street where gardens hide the houses behind. I put on my sunglasses and park the car beside number 34. There is a plaque on the gate. It says 'Fairydell.' I check the address and yes, it's the right number. The only sound is a distant lawn mower. It's so quiet. So calm.

And then I hear a scream which gasps into laughter. And it's like an echo of my laugh. Mine when I was young. I look in the rear-view mirror to find out who the laugh is coming from. And I see her. She has red curly hair and a turned-up little nose. I watch her for a while as she talks with her friends at the gate. And then she swings her satchel over her shoulder and starts to walk up the drive-way. My eyes follow her until she disappears around a bend. Suddenly the road is empty. Suddenly there's silence. Then I get out of the car and walk fast after her. My heels keep getting stuck in the mud and I snag my tights on a bush.

'Josie Brown?' I ask. I'm out of breath. Too much smoke, I suppose.

She turns round and she stares at me, really hard. Her eyes aren't blue anymore but green. I stop in my tracks.

'This is private property,' she says. And her voice is all crips and correct.

'I know that,' I say. 'Listen you don't know me but . . . My name,' I say quietly, 'is Kathy. I knew you when you were a little baby.'

'And my name isn't Josie. It's Tarquinia.'

I am surprised, shocked even. They said they would keep the name. Keep the name, for me.

She looks at me, side on. And then she shrugs.

'Well, what do you want me to do about that?'

I sigh. I take a deep breath but I'm shaking.

'You see.' My mouth opens and shuts like a goldfish. And then it spills out. Just comes out on it's own like a secret streamer of words.

'I'm your mother,' I say.

She stares at me really hard and I swallow, too visibly for my liking. But her little face lights up. She takes two steps towards me. In the fading light, she looks almost angelic, like a vision or a sepia photograph.

'Fan-tastic. I always knew I was adopted. I hate my parents. Have you come to take me away from all this?'

'Well, I just . . .'

'Let me get my things,' she says. 'Do you have a car?'

I nod.

'Wait there and I'll be back in five minutes.'

She starts to run and then she stops and runs back to me.

'Will I meet my real father as well?' she asks.

'Eh . . . perhaps,' I reply and her face breaks into a huge smile and I can see metal braces on her molars.

'Fabby brilliant,' she says.

My heels have stuck fast into the driveway. I pull them out one by one and then walk back to the car. I feel dizzy. I feel very dizzy. The birds sing in the trees and the leaves rustle softly. I see the house through the trees. It's a large pink Georgian mansion with landscaped gardens. I suddenly feel a deep sense of dread. But it passes like a cloud on a sunny day.

There isn't a radio in the hired car, so I start to hum. And then I catch sight of myself in the rear-view mirror and stop. I look ancient and childlike at the same time. I grip the steering wheel. My nail varnish is all chipped and so I start to bite it off, spitting the bits out into the ashtray.

I hear Tarquinia before I see her. Her footsteps echo

as she runs and a large dog barks. It is a golden Labrador. Tarquinia has changed. She wears a black mini skirt, over the knee socks and a green cropped nylon jacket. She carries a bag over her shoulder. She turns to the dog. 'Sit,' she shouts. 'Stay.' The dog obeys, whining slightly.

And then she's in the car, slamming the door and throwing her bag in the back before I know it.

'My parents, I mean my adoptee parents come back around now,' she says. 'I think we'd better step on it.'

I pause, my hand on the ignition key, and the dog starts to bark.

'Come on.' She thrusts her chin at me and I see she's wearing lipstick. Pink lipstick. I push the car into first gear, it shudders, and I drive back into town.

We don't say much on the way. My mind is split between negotiating the traffic and terror at what I have done.

I take her to my favourite restaurant. It used to be a lively place with burgers and steaks, but now it's called Seafood Deluxe. We sit at the back at a table for two surrounded by the green glow of fish tanks. She orders lobster. I order soup and a roll. And Tarquinia talks.

'They stopped my pocket money once,' she says. 'Just because I borrowed five pounds. Five measly pounds. I should have taken fifty. I really needed it for my taxi fare. I mean, do they want me to get mugged coming home from a club? My dad beats me. He does. He beats me when I don't tidy my room. And my mother forces me to wear things. She ties me to a chair until I put on disgusting dresses. With *flowers* and *frills*. You can't let me go back. I'll commit suicide if you do. Like Kurt Cobain.'

Tarquinia doesn't like the lobster – too many creepy bits – so I order a selection of puddings instead. She eats them all. The bill is huge. I pay and then take her home to our house. I can't think of anything else.

The flat looks much worse in the daylight. Damp stains

the concrete on the outside and the yellow glass of the patio door looks like old lemon curd. I park outside. There are plenty of spaces as no one round here has a car. Tarquinia sits in the front seat clutching her bag. Her face is blank but her mouth turns down at the corners ever so slightly.

'Do you live here?' she says in a very little voice.

I look at the flat and suddenly it looks like a slum. I never realised. I didn't notice it before. Because it was temporary, just a place to stay until we got ourselves back on track. We've been living there for seven years in June.

'No,' I say. 'Just come to pick something up. This is a friend's house. Ours is being renovated at the moment.'

'Thank God,' she says. 'There's no way I'm living there.'

I look at her out the corner of my eyes. I see her face in the rear-view mirror. And she's smirking.

'Stay here,' I tell her. 'Won't be a moment.'

Steph still isn't home. I thought he would be. I left a sandwich out for him and it's curled at the edges. I pull a piece of paper from the pile of newspapers on one of the kitchen chairs. It's a bill, but only a blue one. I turn it over and write him a note.

'Steph, you'll have to toast it – don't forget to switch the grill off – remember last time. Something's come up. Don't worry about me. Goodbye. Love Kathy.'

And then I stop in my tracks. I start to panic inside. I grab a cigarette and light it, wondering if I've gone mad and haven't noticed. But I can't go back now. I grab some clothes, shove them into a Tesco bag and put out the cigarette.

I leave my flat with the big bath and yellow glass behind and decide, quite calmly, that I'm never coming back. I slam the door and put the key under the mat. The car sits like an orange omen. Inside Tarquinia is smoking an Embassy Regal. We start to drive to Fife.

'Where are we going now?' she asks.

'To the seaside,' I say and smile like a toothpaste advert.

'Oh,' she says.

'So Tarquinia,' I say. 'Don't you have a nickname or something?'

'God no,' she says. 'At least not Tarquie, or anything gross like that. Some people call me The Snog.'

'Oh, that's unusual,' I reply.

She turns and looks at me again out of those pea-green eyes. And she smirks. Again.

'Usually boys', she says, as she blows smoke up towards the sunshade.

We zoom along motorways and down country lanes. Everything is green and calm and slightly damp. It is only March but it's flat and so vivid. I remember the taste of salt and ice cream. My face in the sun, lying belly down next to the great big earth, feeling the warmth of my own self. When I was whole and new and full of promise. Did I break my own promise? I did. And then I jolt back to the present.

'So, em Tarquinia, em, tell me about yourself. I'm sure there's so much we need to say.'

'What, exactly, do you want to know,' she replies.

'Well . . .'

And I don't know what to say. How can you cram an entire lifetime into a conversation. How can I tell her anything. How can I explain me.

'Doesn't this car have a tape deck?' she asks. 'I've brought some tapes.'

'I, er, don't think so,'

'Don't you know?' she asks. 'It's only your car. It's only your stereo.'

'Well, you know how it is,' I reply, blushing. 'Burglars.'

'My dad has an alarm. My dad has a CD player in his

boot. My dad.' And she suddenly stops. 'Where exactly are we going?' she demands.

'Tarquinia. I know you must think I'm a silly old woman. I know you must be wondering why I gave you away and I'll tell you ... soon. It's crazy, I suppose, but I thought it would be nice to go to the sea alone together. Just for a couple of days. I used to go there when I was your age. And I loved it. I used to find all sorts of things on the beach. Bits of glass, blue and green and sort of turquoise.'

'Oh,' she says.

'I can't help thinking of the beach as the edge which shifts. It isn't one hard line, but a moving, fluid thing. And it gives me hope, sort of. Makes me feel better.'

'You're a hippie aren't you. Oh God, I thought at least you might be a punk. At least they have a bit of street cred. But a hippie.'

'I'm not anything,' I say. 'I just want you to see it.'

'I've seen the sea before,' she says. 'What do you think I am? Deprived? We go to Majorca every year. We even have an apartment. With three bedrooms, two bathrooms, a pool ...'

I pull into a lay-by. I stop the car. I turn to her. And I feel really angry. But I keep my temper. She looks up at me and she looks a little bit scared.

'Do you want to come to the sea with me?'

She frowns and her forehead creases up in the middle. Her lipstick isn't put on straight and a little bit of pink is blurred onto her cheek.

'Yes,' she says in the little voice.

'Right,' I say and pull off again. I don't see the lorry and it blasts its horn at me. She mouths something I can't quite make out.

We arrive in Anstruther at about five and the sea stretches out as flat as a sheet of aluminium. They've pulled down the public toilets and given the whole place a clean but it hasn't changed much. First I stop and buy us both fish and chips and then I drive to the caravan park. I rent number 64 and then find it's right at the back. There is no view of the sea and we look on to the communal bins. I take out our bags and open the door. It's pretty cold inside, but there's a gas fire and a TV. I turn them both on and empty the fish suppers on to two patterned plates.

Tarquinia is still sitting in the car. I call her and she gets out slowly. She looks a bit blank, but she's probably just tired. Then she slams the door, hard, and comes in and starts to eat without taking her jacket off.

That night I can't sleep. The fold-out bed's hard and the wind howls off the sea. I miss Steph. His large mass, his snores and his faint whiff of whisky. I wonder how he is. And then I imagine the Browns. The couple I gave my baby Josie to. They must be worried sick. I feel a wave of guilt wash over me like the tide.

Josie, or Tarquinia is fast asleep on the double bed. Her mouth is open, she dribbles on to her pillow, but she looks so sweet. So innocent with cheeks like freshly risen bread. And I wonder who her father was.

Eventually I fall asleep and I dream weird dreams where I'm climbing in to a conch and getting lost in the big pink curling, swirling horn. And Josie's there too. She's only a little baby but she's still smoking and swearing. And she's bald, like she was when I last saw her, but she keeps asking me to buy her a wig. Demanding I buy her a long red curly one.

The next morning, I realize by the calm of the air, is a Saturday. I think about the gig in the wine bar which I won't have to play and turn over. I pull all the covers off me at one side and a great wisp of air flies in.

'Do you always wear huge big knickers?' this clear little voice says.

I roll over. I almost forgot.

'Always,' I say.

'I don't wear any. I wear a G-string. You should try it. It's much more sexy. If you've got cellulite though, I suppose you have to cover it up.'

She is sitting up in bed, watching me. In front of her is her open bag and I can see a silver quilted make-up bag and a huge bottle of perfume. She pulls it out and she sprays herself with it. I know she expects me to say something, to ask her where she got it or how much it cost. I don't.

I get up and go out for breakfast. I buy butter baps and Nescafe, honey and bacon to give her a choice. It's still windy and the sea whips along the harbour wall. All the fishing boats are out. In the middle of the sea, almost within swimming distance are two islands, I've forgotten the names but they hump there half way to North Berwick like two old reliable friends.

Tarquinia is dressed when I come back. She sits watching the TV with her jacket on as if she's just about to leave.

'Are you hungry?' I say.

'Why? What have you bought?'

She opens the Spar bag and does her blank stare.

'Eh, no thanks,' she says.

So I make myself breakfast and eat it. I can feel the crumbs fall from my chewing mouth and they cascade like polystyrene rocks on to the floor.

We both look out of the window at the bins. A dog is pulling out a half eaten chicken from a bin bag. Somebody in a near-by caravan is watching Scotsport. He cheers and shouts at regular intervals.

'I used to love it here,' I say.

She doesn't reply.

'You know, I haven't been here once for over 20 years. But it hasn't changed, well not much. The women in the bakery is the same.'

I smile and turn to her.

'Isn't that strange?' I say.

Tarquinia just exhales. Loudly. 'I'm bored,' she says. 'I'm so, so, so bored.'

'Well, lets go out. There's so much we have to talk about.'

'I . . .' she says. And she swallows, and then looks at me with a wounded expression.

'You what?'

'I do want to go out. But by myself. Just for a bit. Just so I can think. It's a big thing finding out you're adopted, you know. My life will change. Forever.'

There is a silence and a roar from the next caravan. I pick up my plate and cup and start to wash up. 'Well, I suppose there's lots of questions you want to ask me. But let me tell you this . . . I was happy when I had you. I was really happy.'

The door slams. Tarquinia has gone.

'Don't you want to know anything about me,' I say to the space where she was. 'Aren't you interested at all.'

I wait for her in the caravan. I wait until three in the afternoon and I start to worry. I imagine her falling off the end of the pier. I imagine her cold and hungry and lost. I put on my coat and fasten a note to the door.

The winding streets are empty as I trip along in my high heels and I curse myself for not bringing anything else. I pass a few busy pubs but don't go in. She wouldn't. She might. I go in and have a look. But they're filled with boys in shell suits and old men with pipes. They all stare at me and shout offers of drinks as I leave.

In the main street a few elderly tourists are tossed

around by the wind, their jackets like half-inflated balloons. There are some people waiting for the Glasgow bus who keep squinting into the distance and tapping their feet. And then I see her. She is leaning against the wall outside the chip shop. She holds a bottle of sherry in one hand and a cigarette in the other. A crowd of teenagers, mostly boys, have formed a loose circle around her. They laugh and show off, shouting and punching and interrupting each other. She is the only one with a bottle and she hands it round. Then she pulls handfuls of sweets from her pocket; tubes of Smarties, Mars Bars and Wine Gums.

I watch her from behind the telephone box, conspicuous in my leopard-skin mackintosh, but I can't move. Then one boy lunges at her and tries to take the bottle and she runs away, teasing him with it held above her head. They keep on sprinting and dancing, sprinting and dancing until they reach the beach. I follow slowly at a distance. I don't know what to do.

And then I see that they have started to kiss, a long, grinding kiss as if they are both being operated by an electrical appliance. The bottle falls out of her hand and smashes on the concrete, and then they disappear behind the sea wall. I sit down in the bus shelter. The bus from Glasgow pulls in. Everybody gets on. I keep on sitting.

Half an hour later, I hear the click of her footsteps. I stand up and step out of the bus stop. She gets a fright, gasps when I appear in front of her. We just look at each other. Her with her socks around her ankles and her hair full of sand and me with my bright coat and my angry expression. I stare her out.

'What's wrong with you?' she asks. 'Don't tell me you were a model of virtue at my age.'

She twists her mouth to one side and then thrusts her chin up at me.

'I mean look at you. You look like the tart from hell.

Just my luck. Why couldn't you have been someone glam, rich and exciting. A film star or something. You don't even have a boyfriend. I mean, what kind of a role model are you?'

I don't say anything. Because she's right. I see me right in front of me. Not the child looking for washed up glass on the beach, but the child looking for something much sharper. At twelve I went with a boy called Ronnie. And then there were more. Kenny and Billy and Andy and Jim. Plus others whose names have gone and whose faces sometimes stare out at me from old men begging in the city or from the driving seats of buses or from the waiters in pizza restaurants.

Something inside me wails. Short and high and then long and aching. And then I do something I have never done before. I take one step towards her. And I slap her, hard, right across the face. And as I gasp at what I have done, her hand, sharp with rings and bitten nails strikes back at my cheek. And it hurts. We glare. We shake. We turn and walk.

After five minutes we reach the end of the pier. I decide to throw myself in. Tarquinia just watches as I take my coat and shoes off.

'You're mad,' she says. 'You're completely mad.'

I turn and look at her. The wind is blowing my hair over my eyes and into my mouth.

'I wanted to save you,' I say. 'You begged me to.'

'You didn't,' she shouts. 'You wanted to save yourself.'

And then she turns and starts to walk back along the pier. She doesn't even glance over her shoulder. The sea looks cold. I climb down the metal ladder in my stockinged soles. A couple of little boys watch me from the other side of the harbour. Then a gust of wind lifts my shoes and carries them over the stone edge. I catch one but the other falls with a plop into the sea.

I hobble back to the caravan. On the way I buy some food from the tiny local supermarket. I avoid catching sight of my reflection but the looks people give me are enough.

The TV is blaring but Tarquinia isn't there. Her clothes are scattered all over the floor and her make-up covers most of the fold-downable table. Sweeties wrappers show she's eaten.

I sit, quite still, for ages.

And then there's a knock on the door. I ignore it.

It comes again. Much more forcefully. I open it a crack. It's the lady from the corner shop.

'I'm sorry to bother you,' she says. 'But it's your wee girl. She's been pocketing half ma shop. Chocolate, crisps, cigarettes, even cat food . . . I caught her but she managed to run off.'

I don't know what to say. I can feel my face blanche even under my make-up.

'Can I pay you back,' I ask.

'Aye, but I'm not quite sure what she took.'

I take out my purse. I've only got thirty pounds left after the food and the petrol. I give her twenty. Judging by the amount of wrappers, it's probably right.

'She's barred mind, but I suppose this will do in the meantime.'

I root through her things and find eight packets of cigarettes. I start to smoke them.

And then there's another knock at the door. I ignore it.

'Kathy, Kathy?'

It's Steph. I open the door. He looks around the caravan. He knows. He doesn't say a word. He takes hold of me and he squeezes ever-so gently. My face collapses like a tent.

'I . . . I'm sorry. How did you find me?'

'You're as easy to read as a map,' he says. 'Where is she?'

I shake my head. I can't take my eyes from the floor.

'I hate myself,' I say. And then he starts to kiss me, saying hush, and he holds me so tight I can feel every inch of his body crushing against mine. And we fit together like we've come from the same mould and I feel better. Then he pulls away and looks straight at me.

'Is she like you?'

'No,' I say. 'She's a nightmare. Well, no and yes. Well, yes. You just forget ... what you want.'

Then I hear a loud fizz and whistle. Right above the next caravan is a streak of red smoke.

'Tarquinia,' I breathe. 'Fuck.'

I take off my shoe and we both run down to the harbour. I see her at the end of the pier, surrounded by boys. She is holding an SOS flare in her hand and is dancing to a boogie box. A low buzz comes from further along the coast. The coastguard in his helicopter appears over the headland. All the fishermen have come out from the pubs and they shake their heads in disbelief.

I stand on the pavement with my toes sticking through my tights. Steph looks at me. I nod. He pushes through the crowd and grabs her by the arm. She shakes him off until he manages to shout something in her ear. Then she comes. The coastguard hovers for a few minutes. He looks very annoyed. We walk back to the caravan site through crowds of locals. They stare at us as if we're exhibits in a murder trial. I know I can never come back again. Then one of them hands me a bill. For £500.

'It's a mandatory charge,' he says. 'The coastguard is supposed to be saving lives, not running after juvenile delinquents.' Tarquinia snorts with laughter.

We pack up our things and I pay by cheque for the caravan, knowing it will bounce. Tarquinia sits in the back of the car in silence. Steph and I sit in the front in silence.

'Where are we going now?' she asks.

'We're taking you home,' says Steph.

'Oh,' she says. 'I know you're not my real parents. You couldn't be. You're too young. And you're . . .' She doesn't finish the sentence but the adjectives pile up in my mind.

We pull in the driveway and up to the house. A woman rushes out when she hears the engine. It's not Mrs Brown. Her face looks like it has been washed and tumble dried with bleary eyes and a crumpled up mouth. She makes this sound. A sort of cross between a cry and a groan. Tarquinia jumps out of the car with her long bag over her shoulder. The woman tries to grab and hug her but Tarquinia brushes her off.

'Did you tape *The Word*,' she says.

She pulls Tarquinia's head to her face and smells her hair. She rubs the hair against her cheek.

'Muuum,' Tarquinia says. 'Oh. Bythe way. Kathy and Steph thought I was their child but they made a mistake.'

The woman doesn't hear, doesn't understand. And then she sighs.

'Maybe next time,' sayd Tarquinia.

When Tarquinia has flounced back into her house without a second glance, the woman looks at me. And I can see fourteen years of something which I can't understand. It's like looking into a well, and seeing a rippled reflection in the dark.

And I feel so jealous and yet so relieved. The woman is so shocked she doesn't know what to say.

'I don't suppose you'd like some tea?' she says. 'I'd better ring the police and tell them she's back. She's done this before. But she always comes back eventually. Oh, by the way, I'm Daphne. Daphne Jack. Thank you so much for bringing her back.' And the woman starts to cry, dabbing her face with a tea towel.

'She's a wild one,' says Steph.

I stand looking at the front door. The woman falls in

and out of focus. And I don't know what I except to see or do.

'We love her,' says Mrs Brown. 'And we've done our best.'

And then she swallows and looks straight at me through her eyes.

'Aren't you . . . I've got one of your records somewhere.'

'No, it wasn't me,' I say.

I hang my head and then I get back into the car.

At home Steph runs me a bath. I get in slowly and lie there like a corpse. Then Steph comes in and closes the door. He takes all his clothes off and climbs in too. He takes my hand under water.

'Josie, the little girl, doesn't exist,' he speaks slowly as if he's talking to someone very old. 'She disappeared shortly after you handed her over. The family moved and if she ever looks for you in the future she'll be a grown-up. It's best that way.'

Then Steph washes me all over like a child and then wraps a big warm towel around my body and around my arms until I'm a cocoon. Fastening another towel around his middle he lifts me up and carries me through to the bedroom. And then he throws me on the bed and starts to tickle me. And we laugh until I'm crying. But it's okay. Because he isn't Ronnie or Andy or Billy or any of those others. And we lie on the bed and I feel like I'm belly-side down to the earth again. And I can feel the warmth of my own self inside. And I make myself a promise.

'You're backwards and forwards,' Steph sings softly. 'Backwards and forwards.'

And then we laugh and laugh and the bed turns into one big roller coaster in the dusk, going round and round and up and down, then straightening out and pulling us into the horizon where anything can happen.

BIOGRAPHICAL NOTES

JOHN ABERDEIN was a fisherman/diver on the West coast before teaching English and sea kayaking in Fife, Hampshire and Orkney. His poetry, stories and Scots translation of *Moby Dick* have appeared in *Oar, New Shetlander, Scottish Literary Journal* and *New Writing Scotland*.

LEILA ABOULELA was born in 1964. She lived in Khartoum and graduated from the University of Khartoum. She travelled to London to study Statistics at the LSE and in 1990 moved with her family to Aberdeen. Her work has appeared in *Chapman, Mica, Left to Write* and *Special Reserve – New Writing by Women in Aberdeen*.

BEATRICE COLIN was born in 1963 and lives in Glasgow. She currently works as a freelance journalist and also writes prose, radio and film scripts. Last year one of her short stories was chosen for the Radio 4 *First Bite* festival.

ANNE DONOVAN was born in 1955 and brought up in Coatbridge, Lanarkshire. She studied at Glasgow University and lives in Glasgow where she works as a teacher. Her writing includes both prose and poetry.

MICHEL FABER was born in Holland in 1960, grew up in Australia, and now lives on Tarrel Farm in Ross-shire with his wife and two children. He has worked as a nurse, a cleaner, and a packer of pickles but prefers being a househusband because he can play Captain Beefheart records while doing the dishes.

JONATHAN FALLA writes and nurses in Edinburgh, having lived in many tropical countries. He has written stage plays, films for the BBC, and a study of ethnic rebels in Burma.

PAULA FITZPATRICK was born in Glasgow in 1951. Having graduated from the Glasgow School of Art in 1973, she tried teaching but escaped, and now works as a clerk in the National Savings Bank. Her short stories have been published in *Chapman* magazine and in *Scottish Short Stories 1993*. Her poems have also been included in three anthologies.

LIZBETH GOWANS was born to a shepherding family in the 30s and has lived in many rural areas of Scotland. She now lives in Yorkshire where she is a part-time literature tutor for the WEA. Her work has been included in previous volumes of *Scottish Short Stories* and *New Writing Scotland* and she has had articles published in the *Scots Magazine*.

ANDREW GREIG is a full-time writer living mostly in Orkney and the Lothians. He has written ten books of poetry, mountaineering and fiction, the most recent being *The Return of John Macnab*.

KATHRYN HEYMAN was born in 1965 and grew up in Australia. An award winning poet, her first novel, *The Breaking*, is published by Orion/Phoenix House in April 1997. Kathryn is currently the Scottish Arts Council Writing Fellow in Ferguslie Park. She lives in Glasgow.

LESLIE HILLS is a director of Skyline Film and Television. She has written numerous reviews and articles for the press and for textbooks but 'Pictures of Ivy' is her first acknowledged fiction.

LORN MACINTYRE was born in Argyll and is a full-time writer. She has had many short stories and several novels published.

JOHN MCGILL was born in Glasgow in 1946. He has published a volume of short stories, *That Rubens Guy*, a novel, *Giraffes*, and has featured in a number of anthologies. He is currently working on a novel set in an igloo in the Davis Strait.

CANDIA MCWILLIAM was born in Edinburgh in 1955. She has published three novels, *A Case of Knives*, *A Little Stranger* and *Debatable Land*. She has three children.

G A PICKIN is 43 years old, has a degree in archaeology and lives in Galloway with her partner and twin daughters. Her work appears in several anthologies, but she spends too much time staring out the window at the lights of Belfast and not enough time working.

CHRIS ROBERTS was born in Greenock in 1961 and now works as a press officer in Dundee. He lives with his wife and three children in a Perthshire village where he spends most evenings trying to avoid writing a novel, so far with some success. 'Goodbye, Robbie Tuesday' is his first published story.

RAYMOND SOLTYSEK was born in Barrhead in 1958 and has been writing since 1992. He was the joint winner of the 1994 Glasgow University DACE/Clyde 2 short story competition and has had work published in *Rebel Inc.*, *Chapman* magazine and local anthologies. As well as completing a short story collection, he dabbles in film and stage projects. He lives in Paisley, and performs his work regularly with the local writers' group.

JOHN SPENCE was born in Paisley in 1935. Since 1968 he has lived and worked in the English Midlands. Since retiring from general practice he has started and abandoned one novel and is now working on another. 'My Son, My Son' is his first published fiction.